Starlight City

Radford Lee

Copyright © 2012 Radford Lee
All rights reserved.
ISBN-13: 978-1478375043
ISBN-10: 1478375043

To my wonderful family.

Thanks for all the love and support, which carried me through tough times.

This book is a work of fictitious art. Any semblance to actual people or events is strictly coincidental or unintentional.

CONTENTS

Prelude	1
Chapter 1	4
Chapter 2	12
Chapter 3	18
Chapter 4	23
Chapter 5	33
Chapter 6	43
Chapter 7	51
Chapter 8	59
Chapter 9	73
Chapter 10	83
Chapter 11	89
Chapter 12	95
Chapter 13	104
Chapter 14	112
Chapter 15	120
Chapter 16	130
Chapter 17	136
Epilogue	155

Starlight City

Creation stems from ideas, mere concepts; the realm of the abstract; the border between order and chaos.

Starlight City

Prelude

Sleeping Siren

I'm starting this media stream with my first memory, one that seemed like a nightmare – the last from a former life. Like the saints on Earth sing, the last will be first.

I was stationed on Harmonica, a spaceport city orbiting Earth's terra-formed moon when a warning signal went out. At 23:11, an unidentified ship flashed on the satellite radar, approaching the moon. Cosmonauts at Lunar Six Command tried to make contact but got no response.

It was close to Harmonica's orbit, and my team was assigned to the task. Our stealth pod fit four soldiers; Smiley, Rex, Luvermin and I would infiltrate the ship. We carried Zeta .17 photon burners, special issue; it was our first job together.

We sat with knees bent in limited space, but the pod got us there quickly. With the sun behind us, we skirted the back edge of the moon. Minutes later, a crescent Earth shined before us. We spotted the craft through the glass floor below, built in eccentric architecture I'd never seen. It was a mid-sized ship. White wisps of light scattered across its surface.

"Land us at a good spot," I told Smiley, my pilot beside me. "See that hatch down there?" I pointed. Smiley nudged the steer knob in the armrest console, tilting the pod to hover over the round hatch. He eased us down and touched "R4" on the console. The crawl cylinder extended beneath the pod, attaching to the craft with vacuum suction.

"We're on solid," said Smiley. "Go for it, Black."

I unsnapped the chest belts and crawled over Rex to the back of the pod, slipped on a helmet from the rack and pressed down until it clamped on the neck of my polymer suit. I turned the pressure wheel to open the round pod door and drifted through the cylinder, weightlessly, to the craft's smooth surface.

An insignia on the hatch – a diamond, or an angled square – had gold markings along the edges like cursive Roman numerals. I sliced the lock with the burner and kicked the hatch open; the handle clattered against metal in the dark. Lowering myself into the ship, I was jerked down by my own weight but caught the edge of the hatch. I turned on my helmet light, looking at gridded walls of an empty corridor as I dropped in. Magnets in my liquid shoes clicked against the metal floor. I tapped the CyberNet Link button on my ear.

"I'm in. There's artificial gravity. Watch your step."

Rex dropped in first. His helmet goggles made his eyes huge, creating a cartoonish look behind dreadlocks hanging over his face. Luvermin followed, then Smiley; I led the way through the shadowy corridor, clutching the burner at my ribs. Arched walls gave me the odd sense of walking diagonally. We snaked through the vessel like cells. Corridors branched from our path at each side, yet something drew me onward.

The path opened to a wide chamber where dim rods of light lined a high ceiling. From where we stood, we saw her: the most perfect creature I'd ever physically seen, captured from a fairy tale, it seemed – her naked body elevated on a platform above, floating in a sealed capsule. Foreign markings glowed on buttons and dials under pale light emanating from the fluid inside. We stared, awestruck by the sleeping beauty floating behind the glass. My CyberNet 'Link picked up buzzing sounds from the capsule. Luvermin broke our silent gaze.

"I have to touch her," he said. "She's bloody inconceivable."

He walked through the empty chamber as if entranced, his shoe magnets clicking with each step. No one spoke. We all wanted to touch her. We watched Luvermin climb metal beams jutting from the wall, pulling himself up. He stood before the capsule, sliding his silver gloves over the glass like he could feel on the other side, gazing at the beauty inside his own reflection. The capsule may have been heat sensitive. A dark screen above it pulsed blue, and the glowing liquid quickly drained. Jet-black hair fell to her shoulders like tangled vines. She stood in the empty vial as the liquid dripped from her perfect form.

Luvermin removed his hands but was too mesmerized to remove himself. The glass opened. He stiffened, then inched forward, reached out a hand halfway, hesitated but couldn't pull it back. His glove pressed against her pale cheek, and envy shuddered through me – a strange moment. Rex bit his bottom lip. We glanced at each other, then looked away. Her eyes opened – eyes the color of a supernova – peering through Luvermin like he wasn't even there.

When I saw what was happening, it was too late. Not that it mattered. I tried to yell; my voice was stuck in my throat. Slender arms lifted Luvermin by the neck of his slim suit, his feet dangling. He gurgled; I heard someone pissing through the waste tube on the leg of his suit but couldn't tell which one of us. I just watched, dumbfounded. She squeezed until his neck broke under the pressure. Then, she let go and he fell to the deck.

A childish laugh echoed, which could have been my imagination. She leapt across the wide chamber, landing near us with a much heavier thud than a human could make; the floor quivered. She turned mechanically toward us, her beauty strangely grotesque now. "Anna II" was etched in the groove of her collarbone. Her radiant eyes gazed at me. She came for us. I fired bursts frantically. Her body absorbed the energy, so I switched to shrapnel fire, yelling for my guys to do the same. Shells blasted skin off her shoulder, her jaw and neck, exposing a metallic skeleton. She moved toward us. We kept firing, our backs to the wall, feet planted. She lifted Rex by his rifle – he wouldn't let go – and slammed him hard, breaking one of his legs.

She whirled and struck me across the face. The back of my helmet smacked a wall behind me. I lay there, looking through my shattered mask. I'd never been hit so hard. As I faded, I heard Smiley scream. Shrapnel rattled beyond the chamber entrance in the corridors.

Then, the silence of night.

Chapter 1

*L*ead Eye warned me to stay clear of the one-hundred districts. I didn't listen that night I caught the SkyTram uptown, looking for a nice place with good people – a classic joint, not just a clean, well-lit place.

Stepping off at a Level Three transit station, I took the glass escalator to Level Two. Watching traffic coast down Rune Street fifty stories below reminded me of a rhyme I'd heard in another life, a metaphor about car lights being red and white blood cells. The city was the heart; the cells pulsed through it.

It was late, but Starlight City shined as always. Strolling the air walks in the warm breeze, I felt like a speck on a flea. Cities back home were sort of like this.

A display on a glass cloudscraper flashed, "Breaking News Update." Two modified humanoids owned by the Regime had gone AWOL. Administrator Nahzir would pay gigabytes to anyone who hunted them down. The story had been running for five cycles, was considered old news now.

I pulled the cigar from inside my hood vest to sample the bitter-sweetness on my tongue. A "Quad Star Replica Maintenance" icon shined above the guardrail. At the building's end, I stopped under a "Lover's Lane" sign glowing below the air cart strip, lit the cigar with my Bic and took a puff. An egg-shaped drone drifted silently my way, shined red scanners over me and floated past.

I descended stairs to a fenced walkway as a shiny black cart sped overhead, its humming engine barely audible. I spotted white walls on rubber tires folded underneath.

At the next air walk, a good-looking couple stepped from a tinted walk bridge branching from an island above Commerce Circle. They had on fancy silver cloaks. The guy, wearing a jet-black fedora and shades darker than mine, locked arms with the girl as the breeze fluttered her copper hair and checkered scarf, worn for style, I assumed, since the weather was nice. She was light brown with freckles. Her lips formed a smirk as he mumbled something.

Another man led a tiny dog onto the island platform across the walk bridge. The dog sniffed the edged grass where two lovers embraced on a stone bench beside a mulberry tree. The decorative benches surrounded a black pearl fountain, which spurted thin jets of water in front of the Earth Museum. Sparkling lights on the fountain illuminated their faces.

Folks sure seemed happy around here. For the first time since waking up on Planet Neon, I began to feel homesick.

Around the corner, trumpets on a display to my right spouted rainbow sixteenth notes. Through an open door beneath them drifted laid-back sounds of a sax playing a smooth jazz number.

I passed the club. Another next to it had its doors closed, and techno-bass thudded inside. I recognized the song and actually cracked a smile. "I wear my sunglasses at night." The song was describing me.

A star-flecked sign flashed, "Milky Way Bar and Café" across the air-walk bridge. It looked inviting, so I crossed to the other air-walk.

Bells jingled as I pushed the door open. The bouncer flashed a platinum grin and said, "Come on in." Rows of green and red glasses twinkled under dim lights behind the bar. A few people sat at the nearest end. I headed to the far side, sliding my hand along the rail separating the bar from the mostly empty dining area, running my fingers over the aged wood.

There were vacant barstools near a gleaming white piano in the back corner. A sharp fellow in a black tux and white necktie sat at the keys playing the end of a soft, sad song. The jukebox display flashed, *Back Down Memory Lane*, in blue lights. On top of the piano sat a classy lady wearing a cream dress and flowers in her frizzy hair, singing to the lucky fool, gazing at him with honey-brown eyes.

They were both holos, but still so lifelike it was hard not to believe they were right there in the flesh.

"What's on your mind, pal?" asked the bartender, a large man with a sleeveless jacket. His left arm was covered with tribal tattoos.

"I'll do a Blue Moonshine over dry ice," I told him. "Double it up for me, man."

"Sure thing," he said.

When the song ended, a lonely old lady in a straw sunhat stood from the table behind me, sliding two shiny tokens into the coin stand beside the holo. The pianist played softly at the keys again, and the lady in cream started humming this melody. The tune was so familiar.

"That song," I said, surprised at the memory. "My mother used to sing it all the time, when I was home."

"That so?" asked the bartender, twisting braids in his gray goatee. He slid the smoking glass to me. "Strange. Never heard the machine play that one before. It has that vintage feel."

"You'd bet your ass, it does," I said. "This is classic."

I turned my stool to lean against the bar and sip from my shiny glass, watching the beautiful woman on the piano sing that song – letting her voice take me far out.

La la la la la…La la la la la…
La la la la la…La laa laa laa…

God, those sunny days.

This place ain't so bad after all, I thought as the song faded.

"Can't remember who sings that," I said. "It feels like ages since..." since I could recall that other life with such clarity.

The doorbells chimed, and two armed patrols walked in wearing light armor with headgear visors flipped back. Maybe I spoke too soon. I turned around, took the last hard swig and motioned for the bartender.

"Need another one?" he asked. I nodded. He reached beneath the counter, grabbed two bottles and poured them. The liquor steamed the ice. He slid the glass to me, glanced over my shoulder and leaned in discreetly.

"Hey, buddy," he whispered. "Don't look now. Them guards are staring at you." I nodded again. Moments later, a hand grabbed my shoulder.

"Pardon, city walker," said a friendly voice. "I need to see your barcode, please."

"What's that?" I asked without turning around. I took a sizeable swig of the moonshine, savoring the sting in my chest.

"I need to see identification." He spoke louder and tugged my shoulder, turning me slightly. I craned my neck to see him – an older guy, late forties maybe, with dark eyes and a clean shave. Four diamond insignias with strange characters were sewn over the pectorals of his black uniform. I'd seen the design somewhere.

"Let's see that barcode," he repeated. "Or an ID badge." I reached for my wallet.

"Is there some issue?" I asked.

"An ID scan near this district came up blank," said his partner, a younger, blonde man. "The patrol sent us a snapshot – and it's your picture."

Of course I knew what the problem was. My fake ID hadn't scanned. It was the second time I'd had this problem. I reached into my hood vest, found my wallet and opened it for them to see. The older one took a scanner from his belt and put a gloved finger to his ear, sliding his black visor down.

"We'll make sure it checks out and be on our way," he said through his muzzle as he scanned it. This time it worked. He paused, maybe reading something on his visor, and slid it up, nodded and handed the ID back. "He's clean. Sorry to bother you, sir. Enjoy the evening."

His partner narrowed intense blue eyes. "Jim, can you really tell that's his ID?" he asked. "Can hardly see his face. Sir, remove those glasses, please."

I froze.

"You heard what I said, man. Take the damn glasses off. You speak alien code?"

We stared each other down. Removing my shades was the last thing I wanted to do.

"Let's not do this tonight, pal." He snatched the shades off my face. "Who the hell wears sunglasses at night?"

"I heard that song on my way here." I said. "You can't hear that song and not put your sunglasses on. That's a crime."

"You think you're an entertainer? You'd better watch your . . ." he paused, bewildered. "Those are freakish eyes you've got, pal. I've never . . ."

"Paul, wait," said Jim, the older one, grabbing Paul's shoulder. "He's not . . ."

"Holy . . . " was Paul's reply. "He's modified. He's one of those . . ." They reached for their burners. I smashed the pretty glass into shards on patrolman Paul's face and slid off the stool, shoving him over the rail. He crashed through the table behind us. The old woman shrieked and fell back, losing her hat. I caught the barrel of Jim's burner as he aimed, twisted his arm and smacked his face against the edge of the bar, chucked the burner toward the back wall and shoved him down.

"Not trying to fight," I told them, snatching my shades off the floor and putting them on. I dug in a front vest pocket and laid a handful of kilobyte tokens on the bar. "Sorry about this," I said, and I was. The bartender shook his head.

"Bullshit. It's nothing," he said with a wave. "Everyone's welcome at the Milky Way." I stepped over Jim and made haste for the door as Paul crawled to his burner.

"Call for backup," I heard Jim mutter. "He might be the alpha human."

"One of those freaks killed my crony," Paul yelled. "You think I'd let him run off?" His burner cracked the reinforced glass door as I ducked out, hoping to slip away, but luck wasn't on my side just then. I almost wondered if she might be bitter about the times I took her for granted in the other life.

Another guard in an armored suit stood on the air-walk just outside with a cannon on his shoulder harness. The word "Sentinel" was etched along the barrel. He must have been waiting all day for something to go down. As he spotted me, I broke into full sprint down the air walk. The guy had dead-eye aim. The blast exploded into my shoulder, and the world spun as I barreled across concrete and metal. Intense pain throbbed in my shoulder. I lay there, looking for my right arm; it was blown off completely. I bled onto the air walk as someone screamed hysterically. A young lady stood over me near the guardrail, clutching her pink handbag, frozen with shock. Commuter cart horns buzzed distantly below.

Not letting the pain slow me down, I staggered to my feet and kept running. The blood was already clotting.

Sirens wailed as I turned the corner at Fifth and Goodkirk. A crowd stood at a sky transit station beside the "North 24" signpost that flashed tram arrival times. I pushed through the startled people. Someone yelled, "Stop," as I rushed along the Level Two air walk, looking over the guardrail. Sloped spires rose from an old chapel on the street level. Without thinking, I climbed the rail, leaping for the closest one. The drop was higher than it looked. I slammed against the slope, failed to grip the grainy surface and tumbled back, smacking the roof hard and rolling to the edge with the wind knocked out of me. Commuter carts sang in my ears as I gasped for air.

Conjuring strength, I rolled off the roof and landed on concrete stairs below. Four granite statues with eagle's heads and wings were hunched at either side. I tried the rusty door at the top of the stairs with no luck and jumped the banister, rushing around overgrown bushes along the neglected lawn to the side of the chapel.

It's hard to say how I scaled the wall with one arm, but I crawled to a stained glass window and kicked through, grabbing the ledge on a parapet above and swinging into a dark room. I Leaned out the window, looking toward the street as four masked guards and two drones rushed by.

"He jumped down this way," one said. "Heaven's holiday, that freak was fast. But I shot the bastard."

"Where's the blood trail?" another one asked.

"Who in hell knows? There was only a puddle where I blew off his arm."

My heart pounded relentlessly. I couldn't help uttering, "Jesus Christ," as their voices faded. They hadn't seen me.

I looked around the small room, which was like a dusty attic; a few antique pianos were clustered in the center, and an organ sat against the wall. Everything was caked with dust. The place clearly hadn't been used in years – a good spot to lay low a few days while my arm regenerated.

Sitting on a wobbly piano bench, I looked out the busted window. Beyond tall evergreens at the edge of the lawn, signboards gleamed on rooftops. A wide screen near the top of Denizen's Hall played NewStream Daily posts from net page subscribers. One was a text loop called, "E-Streams Extracted," an e-journal by some guy named Tom Hurst.

Two moons were visible in the starlit sky, one a lurid green, the other waxing pearl. I imagined Earth was up there somewhere, and wondered what it looked like – a colorful star, maybe.

To be honest, I missed that other life, but I couldn't get it back. Must have been by some miracle that I even made it to this rock they called Neon – something that trumped impossible odds, like the Big Bang. Maybe Lady Luck did care, or someone did. I was alive, and at that moment, I decided to make the most of it. Thank God I was always an optimist. It was taxing on my inner peace, being hunted every day, but I was built to survive.

E-Streams Extracted
Log-001..

    The Kepris virus spread via the CyberNet® -- an anomaly that seeded from nowhere, like how the fly spawns from the decay it feeds on. The bug corrupted systems in factories owned by Zahncorp Pharmaceutics, causing the drones that process their drugs to create high concentrations in small doses. Lots of people died that way.
    News feeds headlined it "The Beautiful Death." Few infected have survived. One man whose internal respirator was invaded by the virus reported seeing iridescent colors flittering from the sky like loose strands of a rainbow. Others reported similar symptoms. On the main feeds this morning, a woman said she saw winged angels in rays of sunlight, walking amongst people.
    I wonder if Griffin saw them. The audio files from that ThinkCap© Anna bought him for Leap Day are on my StarMack interface. I thought it was a silly toy until he showed me how it could record his logical thought processes; he even altered the coding so it played them back in an auto-tuned voice. He was wearing it when he tried to kill himself. I can't listen to it.

                      Thomas Hurst -- NewStream Daily

Chapter 2

I walked across massive drainpipes beneath the shore walk one drizzly Odin's Night, with "Walking in the Rain" streaming through my mind. It's strange how I remembered old songs. Music has always been a thing for me.

Several times I'd crossed these pipes, pretending they were the entrails of Starlight City, draining its souls into the sea.

Whenever I walked this path, the chorus to a certain song popped in my head:

> *What happened to that soul brothers used to talk about?*
> *Everybody's shallow now. Man, everybody's shallow now.*

Lead Eye would say "hollow" instead of "shallow." He called this place Hollow City, "Not because there's holos everywhere you turn," he'd said, "It's 'cause most these people don't have souls."

I felt like a wayward soul myself, drifting through timeless space.

Rain splashed loud on the dock that lay beyond the sea wall where the pipes ended. The solar boats bobbed with the tide.

Mounting the sea wall edge, I climbed into a sewer passage

beneath the Café Shack, splashing puddles and following snake-like power beams throbbing with pristine light along the ceiling. The beams pumped Omega, the city's lifeblood, to traffic lights and buildings on the surface.

Tangerine light from the Café Shack shined through a slatted storm drain, making halos in some plastic bottles I kicked with hollow clunks.

Up ahead, a pale glow illumined graffiti etchings on the concrete wall. One abstract design I liked to call "The border between order and chaos" resembled something different each time I saw it. This time it was a colorful sphinx with curved talons.

Lead Eye's chain gate was pulled taught around iron pipes. A steel rod on a pad lock ran through each loop. I rattled the chains. Lead Eye peeked cautiously around a corner, loose dreadlocks dangling over his right eye. The blue scan lens in his left socket was trained on me. I suddenly recalled a guy named Rex I once knew on Earth, maybe because Rex had dreadlocks too.

"You?" He cackled dryly. "Told you to meet me seven revs and thirty-one thousand, three hundred forty-eight ticks ago. What happened to you, Black?"

"Ran into trouble," I told him. He reached through the chains with a key and unlocked the gate.

"What'd the devil do to your hand?" He touched the end of my sleeve.

"Nothing."

"You're damn well right it's nothing," he laughed again, locking the gate as I stepped into the humble abode he'd recently claimed. A round bulb hung from wires wrapping an Omega beam on the ceiling. He'd furnished the place with two corroded metal drums that said "Petroleum." A plastic, green tote sat between them, and a silver space heater spun beside an air mattress at the back.

"What'd you do?" he asked, sitting on the drum furthest from us. I took the nearest one.

"You don't want to know."

"Ain't go uptown, did you?" The human eye behind his dreads peered at me. "Told you not to. Be wise and steer from trouble, or end up a mutilated freak like me."

"That's not the half of it," I mumbled to myself.

"That's what I mean," he replied, pointing a bandaged finger to the streets above. "City walkers don't like some halfling running around." The pupil inside his green eye dilated. "Net search famous faces," he said. "Chat with a prosthetics specialist about cosmetic upgrades today."

"Do what?" I asked, confused.

"Who's that now?" he looked at me with a frown. "Ahh." He shook his wooly hair, slapped his metal hand against the metal plate in his skull. "Network signals crossing my brain waves – since that Kepris outbreak. It did something weird to my 'Link."

I tried to remember what outbreak he meant. My burning, itching wrist distracted me.

"I need a new ID," I told him. "Know where I can find Hodge? She wasn't at the shop."

"Hodge got out of Dodge. You ain't heard?" He looked surprised. "It's been on holos at every transit station," he said. "Regime soldiers caught some underground terrorists that shot up a university lab. Hodge was the one sold them the weapons.

I wasn't sure what to say.

"Unfortunate," I blurted. An understatement. Hodge wasn't just a mutual friend; she was the source of our livelihood.

"She's got connects in West Four-Nineteen, the wall district. Bet they'll find her soon, though. Can't get nothing past them."

"Four-Nineteen?" I repeated.

"Better find her quick. You won't last without a badge. They'll get after you."

"Too late."

"Too what?" His blue lens focused in and out. "Well what'd you come here for? You'd think I had enough problems." He rolled up a ratty coat sleeve, tapped the 'Link screen on his metal arm. "You seen this?" He touched icons to play a streaming clip of a quasi-man – the torso awkwardly attached by brackets to metal legs – holding his arm around the throat of a smaller, fully human man, pointing a burner at the man's head. Armed citizen guards in the background had weapons aimed.

"That psycho Nahzir has the GenPub eye out for quasi-humans. I ever tell you about them human killing machines they were building when I was a soldier?"

"Alpha humans?" I remembered. He nodded slowly.

"Bet he's looking for parts," he said with contempt. A message flashed on the screen summoning all quasi-humans in Starlight City to Nahzir's Gate for debugging.

"I'm leaving," I assured him, standing. "Thanks for the lead."

"Come back when you're clean. I'm getting more cigars from the delivery kid. Better than the last ones. He says the leaves are fresh from the greenhouse market."

"Looking forward to them," I said.

I jumped from the sea wall to the dock where aqua lights lined the polished wood, passing long rows of solar sailboats in the misty drizzle. At the far end, an electronic fence sectioned off the naval port. A freighter glowed at sea between phosphorescent buoys some distance out from the coast. Its massive searchlight pierced the gray night, skimming the water.

Not searching for me. Of course not.

Dark pyramids floated on the water, and a steel curtain blocked the rest of the beach.

Stairs led me to the shore walk on Seaside View where commuter carts hummed by, splashing raindrops stained in reflected light. City walkers rushed by with hoodies or cloaks covering their heads, stepping gingerly over puddles. Some strolled under colorful umbrellas. Across Seaside View, a cylinder of LED screens towered the curving street.

The South Main transit station sat on the next block. I couldn't ride the trams without ID, so I squeezed through a crowd of dockworkers. Their dim faces looked drained as they waited quietly for the StreetTram.

The AutoBus stop was below the SkyTram terminal, where thousands of feet scattered across the glass platform. I sat nearly ten spins on a heated bench, glancing up to watch trams glide in from the west districts before an AutoBus whistled to the curb. The display on the top deck read "Northbound." Hodge's spot was on the west end, so I figured I'd wait for a westbound ride, then changed my mind when I saw a patrol drone floating toward me.

I hopped on the Auto as it started off, climbing the stairs to an empty seat beside the traffic. A bored looking kid was slouched in the seat across the aisle, typing on a handheld 'Link device with his thumb. His eyes hid behind a visor attached to his big headphones.

The drone hovered like a fat metal hummingbird, running scanners over the bench where I'd just sat. A lens under its translucent shell shifted in all directions, and slowly turned on me. I ducked as the Auto sped up to merge with traffic.

On the seat in front of me, I punched "W-4-1-9-#" on the GPS. A section of the Diamond, a steel and concrete wall surrounding most of Starlight City, lit up near a "P1" icon. The counter on the screen said it would be a few revs, but it would take me to the west end.

I sighed, gazing down the brilliant street. A neon clock glowed a couple blocks down. Its white numbers formed a diamond shape. The rev hand leaned toward "sixteen" lined even with "one" at the top – half-past thirty-one hundred, Odin's last hour. Hopefully, I'd find Hodge before sunrise.

The Auto eased around a curve. I leaned against the rail, pulling my hood over my face, and for the first time in three days, dozed off.

Starlight City

E-Streams Extracted
Log-002..

    Beanie at the Cryogenics College pulled some strings so I could keep Griffin in their preservatory. The medics said he wouldn't make it; I know he's alive still, just barely. His brain won't tell his body to eliminate the toxins. The challenge for us is compiling an anticode to mimic a cure for the illness the virus simulates.

    Griffin was infected through a software update for his ThinkCap©; his mind was altered. As far as we could tell, his A-conscious was nullified, his C-conscious enhanced. But I don't see how that made him try to kill himself. Maybe I'll listen to that ROM data...tomorrow. I've wasted too much time daydreaming – though dreams invade the consciousness when you haven't slept in days.......

Thomas Hurst -- NewStream Daily

Chapter 3

Someone's hand shook me awake.

"This your stop?"

Instinctively, I slapped the arm and tried to grab the sleeve, forgetting I didn't have a hand to grab with, just a growing bulge, like a plant illusively unfolding. The woman looked sorry she'd disturbed me. Her smooth skin and soft features said early to mid-twenties in Earth cycles, but her eyes held the wisdom of age.

"My lapse, miss," I said. "Bad dream."

"No worries." She seemed relieved. "You should have that worked on." She nodded at the missing hand. "I know an amazing specialist."

"This?" I said. "Don't worry. I'll get along."

The woman smiled understandingly.

"Still." She handed me a clear, flimsy card. Images appeared at my fingertips – an alluring virtual woman posed with bared breasts. A naked man posed beside her, his muscles shapely, as if carved from bronze. Shiny letters above them said "Neuron Prosthetics."

"A fairly simple procedure, to get a hand made," she said. "Dr. Merlo's the name."

"Thanks." I slid the card into my wallet, hoping it would please her enough, and stepped off.

The Auto left me at the curb of an empty street. There was no transit interval there. I hadn't known the wall district could only be reached via SkyTram. Someone could fly an air cart up there, I supposed, but only famous faces owned them, and no famous face would be caught dead in the wall district.

Most residents on the wall were alleged criminals who'd survived citizen justice, or people like Lead Eye, mechanically altered with too many parts that weren't human. Only wall residents who weren't "diseased" or "accidentally mutated" had clearance to even ride the trams. Hodge said some mutations were from being too close to the Ether Shield that wraps Starlight City in a sterilized bubble.

The rain had stopped. To my right, cloudscrapers lined the city limits. Clean white pavement extended on my left and stretched to steel beams of the Diamond, a steel wall that encircled Starlight City. It was a fourth the height of the cloudscrapers near it. About half a mile down where the wall vanished behind other tall buildings was a big "419" painted in black.

Beads of water trickled down the gray steel beams, reflecting LED screens on buildings behind me. I slid my hands across the wet surface, looking up. A silver SkyTram coasted along a track above me.

It was quite a climb.

I was out of breath as I reached the top, the microfibers in my palms and fingertips loosing clinginess. Grabbing the high fence along the edge, I felt a surge of strength, wedged my shoe through a gap and climbed over.

A dark-skinned, skinny little girl in purple leggings stood beside a mammoth canine to my right. Each stared toward the cloudscrapers, watching ads flash on the screens. The girl's pink hat had a fluffy ball on the end; her rainbow-colored hair was spread across her coat collar. A C-shaped 'Link device with blue lights was clipped to her ear.

The wolf's furry ear flipped toward me as I leaned on the fence to catch my breath.

"You climbed way up here?" the girl asked. The wolf looked curious too, cocking its head.

"Sure," I breathed, finding a cigar in my pocket.

"Can you teach Augie to do that? He don't listen to me. I tried teaching him to fly like Zero from the holo show, but alls he did was lick stuff." Augie approached as she said this, sniffed my shoe and licked it.

"Sorry," I said with the cigar in my teeth. I took off my shades to wipe them with my sleeve. The girl wasn't shocked at my yellow eyes, clearly visible in the flashing lights. I was surprised when the lights hit hers. The irises were multicolored prisms.

"I'm looking for a friend," I said.

"The wizard?" she asked. Augie thumped his thick tail against the weathered concrete.

"Huh? No, just a woman." I walked along the fence, noting a sign that read "high voltage." They walked alongside me. Augie was nearly my height on all fours.

"What kind of woman is she?" asked the girl. "A tin woman?" I shook my head. "A brown woman?"

"She is a brown woman, actually."

"What's she look like?"

I paused. How to describe her? "Blue-streaked hair, usually wears a ThinkCap." Not much for the kid to go on. City walkers wore their hair in lots of colors, and wore all sorts of StarMack accessories and 'Link attachments. "Never mind. I think she's hiding."

"Bet she's in the secret club."

I asked what she meant.

"My pop goes to this secret club every night," she said. "Augie and me are gonna find it. We're on a mission."

"Really?" I looked at her. "Is he there tonight?" She nodded. "Maybe my friend's there," I said. "But you don't know where this club meets."

"It's a secret," she grinned with tiny, perfect teeth.

"Of course." I walked on, moving toward a "West 419" signboard near the SkyTram platform. They followed.

"I think Augie knows," she said.

"Yeah?" I stopped again.

"Show him, Augie." She stood in front of Augie, ruffling his huge ears and touching her nose to his. "Can you find Pop? Come on, let's find Pop, Augie." The wolf barked, sniffed the ground and scampered off with the girl skipping behind him. Reluctantly, I trailed them.

The SkyTram platform was usually deserted, except twice a day when the West-17 made routine stops. Other trams had to be programmed manually to stop here. I did spot a drunk in a windbreaker jacket staggering near the platform, gritting his teeth each time he took a sip from his flask. He stopped to squint at a paper comic the wind had blown against the fence.

The prism-eyed girl trailed Augie between vendors' crates containing packaged foo, thrift clothing, discarded talismans or other random trinkets. Two older men with red faces casually browsed through clothes piled in a crate under a plastic awning.

Not wanting to lose my lead, I sped up the pace.

Brick housing units sat along the inner and outer walls of the Diamond surface. Space heaters rested between every few units; their fans blew heat into the damp night. Aluminum pipes branched from each furnace, poking through unit walls so families could get heat.

Some units were big enough for several families. Iron chimneys emitted smoke from rooftops. A savory smell hung on the air, salt and lemon – fish singed in a kettle maybe.

Augie stopped near a weathered unit with boarded windows, sniffing patches of grass growing through cracks in the cement. Along the outer wall at a gap between units, the surface was cracked and shattered. The top of the steel beam was warped in one small section.

"What happened to the wall here?" I wondered.

"Pop says a missile smashed it."

"A missile from where?" I asked.

"Hey, he found something. What is it, Augie?" Augie circled restlessly near the warped edge.

"Down there?" She pointed. The rain began pouring once more. She looked beyond the city toward a black horizon as lightning streaked above endless Forests far off.

"Whoa boy. Pop said not to get my shoes soaked, Augie. Let's get back."

She promptly turned and ran, skipping around puddles; Augie barreled ahead of her.

"Bye, mister."

They faded in the downpour.

E-Streams Extracted
Log-003..

The Regime wants to confiscate Griffin for testing. There's a load of flotsam. Like Nahzir and his uber-freak friends can create anything that isn't destructive. I knew the Regime was behind the virus and the whole damned ordeal. This proves it. How else could a virus appear from nowhere within the CyberNet®? They're the ones controlling it.

I'll die before I let them take him...... Bless it, get your bearings, Tom. Think. I'll need a plan Y, in case plan X fails. If we can't compile an anticode before they take his body, I'll need a new wheel...

That reminds me; on my way home today, I saw a Stargazer©, one of those rickety fortune telling machines, rolling along the cobblestone path in front of my house. I was a kid when those things were constructed. The bulging white eyes and rubbery face give me the jeebs. Haven't seen one in light years. Thought they'd been done away with once the public lost interest. It still creeps me out, but I'll try anything at this point if it means finding answers.

Thomas Hurst -- NewStream Daily

Chapter 4

Rain pouring off my soaked hood drowned the cigar stub in my fingers. I flicked it away and knelt at the edge of the wall to get a better look. The damage had left a manhole-sized gap above the warped steel. Glancing around first, I hung down over the edge and squeezed inside.

With my only hand, I dangled above a narrow space, drying my face with my other sleeve. Dropping onto the broken concrete beneath me, I eased along the ledge. Thick orange cords, carefully twisted around the end of it, dangled through a jagged hole in a sloped metal surface below; something had smashed through it. Jade light shined within.

I slid down, dropping into a room below. To my surprise, Hodge and two others sat on wooden crates. The source of the light, a satellite map of Starlight City, shined on the wall behind them. Three bunks with plastic mattresses hung from the adjacent wall.

A man on my right pointed a long, chrome pistol at my nose. Red cornrows poked from his gray skullcap.

"Better pray to God," the gunman grunted. "Trespassers ain't spared, I'm afraid."

My eye met Hodge's directly across from me, seated on the far crate. The ThinkCap she wore was plugged into a model lighthouse on the floor, which had a glass eye on top projecting the map.

"Black?" Hodge said, standing. "Hey, he's alright." She waved at the gunman.

"You know him?"

"Put it down, Ike." Hodge stepped slowly toward me, like she thought I might be a ghost. "How in Eternity did you find me?"

I took off my hood. "A four-legged friend."

"Jesus," she said, scratching her wavy, blue-streaked hair. She readjusted the wire clamps on her ThinkCap. A silent man in a gray cloak sat beside her. His head was lowered.

"I wouldn't worry too much," I told her, stepping into the light. "Just a little girl's dog. Hear you're in a jam though."

She shook her head. "Those pole jerkers."

"Language, friend," the cloaked man uttered, his head still down.

"Sorry, Deacon. See Black, I sell off-the-market weapons, to chimera hunters mostly. But these jerk offs buy artillery from me and shoot up a God...blessed public facility. Excrement for brains."

"Seriously," Hodge went on, "A university lab? If you're that bold, why not head straight for the Zenith? That's where things get real interesting. Anyhow, now they're after me, to make a long one short. What about you? How's that bitch Luck treating you, Black?"

"Need a new badge," I told her. "Mine was compromised."

"You're screwed," said the gunman.

"Shut up, Ike," Hodge said. "Sorry, Black. I'd make you another, but you'd have to get my StarMack from the shop. Can't show my face on the surface."

I wasn't sure how I'd find anything in her shop. Twice I'd gone by trying to track her down. The first time things looked fine. When I returned the next day, it looked like a hurricane had stopped by to trash the place. Shelves that held her mechanical toys were smashed, and gadgets lay in piles on the floor. Broken tools and toys were scattered everywhere.

"I think someone cleaned you out," I said. She muffled a curse, kicking an empty tin can behind her seat.

"Should have figured," she said. "There's this other guy they call the Wizard, deep underground. Someone probably made him up though."

"Wow, that helps," I replied.

"Wait, maybe you can help me clear my name," she said. "Ike

was just suggesting we frame someone else. I need to figure how to pull this off."

"Seriously?" I asked. She sat on the crate again, rubbing her fingers to her temples.

"Just let me think some." She closed her eyes. I waited.

"She might be a while," said Ike, rubbing his neck with his burner. "Guess you're alright – boss lady's friend and all. Wait until you see what's inside this place."

In the far corner of the room was another crate, which Ike slid from the wall. A ladder extended to a room below. The cloaked man stood, looked at me and smiled. His loose hood framed his thin, walnut colored face. He was a youthful man but had distinguished wrinkles at the corners of his eyes.

"I'll join you," he said. "Could use a good walk." He passed me in the shadows. Hodge didn't move, so I followed with curiosity, climbing into an identical room below. Ike fumbled blindly for one of the crates in front of him. He reached in and found three fluorescent penlights, handing one to Deacon, who switched it on and pushed the rusted metal door open. Ike held one out for me.

"I don't need it," I said.

"You gagging me?" he asked. "It's pitch dark down here."

"I'm good, buddy. Is this the way?" I walked through the door onto a wide balcony that lined the outermost wall. In dark, everything was shady gray. Moving toward the rail, I could see one balcony above us, and others stories below, all vanishing behind the Diamond's inner wall dozens of doors down.

Ike shined his light in front of us. Deacon pushed through another door further down.

"This place is an armory," Ike told me. "There's a tram station down there too." He pointed his thumb toward the rail to signify "down there" before following Deacon inside the next room with identical wall bunks. "Nothing works, though," he added.

"Regime soldiers stayed in these barracks?" I asked.

"Nahzir has no clue about this place," he replied. That seemed impossible. I'd been under the impression that Nahzir controlled everything in Starlight City, like the grand puppet master.

"You're not serious." I said.

"The Diamond was here before the city was even built," Deacon cut in as Ike pried the top off a crate. "They say it only took ten years to build this city. Nahzir's father landed his ship inside and started building without a second thought about what might be inside this thing."

"It just looks like a huge wall," said Ike, setting his flashlight down and reaching into the crate. "We never knew either, until recently. Been living on top of it all these cycles."

"Why would someone build an armory in a big diamond?" I asked them.

"Something inside the diamond," Deacon suggested, "Like an ancient city. Maybe this was someone's sacred land."

"Maybe Nahzir found an Omega generator," Ike suggested. "There are three in this base. The Regime couldn't have made them." I'd wondered how Omega could power everything in such a massive city.

"How'd you get inside this place?" I asked, thinking about what that little girl had said.

"Used to be housing units where that chunk of the wall is smashed up above," Ike answered. "Debris from Harmonica's missile strike against the Regime – ten cycles ago, I think it was. Most got destroyed by the deflection system, but one got through."

The word "Harmonica" struck a chord. My blood raced as the memory took form. Harmonica was Earth's capital city, orbiting the moon where I'd trained as a soldier.

Ike dug through the crate.

"Citizen Reps never considered having it repaired," he continued. "No one gives two bytes about us rejects on the wall."

"But that missile was a blessing in disguise," said Deacon. "Folks living in the units that got destroyed weren't home at the time. And look." He shined his light on an AA-12 shotgun Ike had pulled out. Ike tossed it to me. It was loaded.

"Old-school burners," Ike said. "There's army carts down there, too," He pointed with his thumb again, "By the old tram system. Come and see."

"Sure."

Putting the weapon back, I followed them along the balcony. They stopped at a gated lift car not far down. Ike slid the gate open and we stepped on. The control panel at the back was covered in dust webs.

"Does it work?" I wondered doubtfully.

"It's battery powered," said Ike. "Just needs a jolt." From the cap of his penlight, a screwdriver extended. He touched it to circuits where the cover was removed, tightening something. Sparks popped. Deacon flipped a lever and lights flickered. We were jostled, then, eased downward as the car screeched along the track. White-hot currents rippled through cables in the wall behind us where the car slid along.

The whining ceased as we hit ground level. We stepped off, and I glanced up at steel columns stretching from the floor and anchoring each balcony.

A tall dome of darkened screen panels sat directly ahead. Cables ran from the dome along the floor every which way. Some reached the steel columns along the balconies. Others drew straight lines up the inner wall to unpowered round lights.

"If we could work these generators, we could power this place," said Deacon. "Hodge goofed around with this one. She says it rusted out."

"You say there's three of these?" I asked.

Ike nodded. "One at the north apex, one at the east."

"Why is there so much Omega around?" I blurted. They glanced at each other, perhaps thinking it strange that I didn't know.

"Generators convert gravity to electricity," Deacon answered. "Magnetism is involved, but I can't explain it much beyond that."

"It's like a water wheel," Ike said, walking toward it. "Have a look."

We ducked through an opening in the dome and stood inside. A large metal wheel was suspended from thick beams twenty feet above. Wires branched from the beams, spreading out behind circuit boards of the thin screen panels. The rusted wheel had twelve steel anchors around its circumference. Metallic discs along the ceiling were lined evenly with the wheel.

"The anchors would spin the wheel if this thing was activated," Ike said. "Hodge was trying to build a small one like this in her shop. I looked at the plans for it. The math looked pretty hairy."

"Physics," Deacon corrected. "The disks up there are magnets that help it spin."

"Yeah, physics," Ike said. "Can't see how she keeps it all straight, even with a ThinkCap. I ain't the smarter offspring, Black, if you can't tell."

Stepping out of the generator, we passed large industrial doors. Terrain maps stretched the walls beside them. Beyond those, dozens of carts with mounted guns were parked side by side.

We climbed into one, and Ike touched his penlight screwdriver to wires hanging behind the wheel, zapping the cart to life. Deacon drove it over tracks toward a row of ancient-looking trams. The cars had faded from what might have once been shiny red or blue. There was no way to tell. Even under Deacon's penlight, they were still gray. Dust and grime collected at corners of the windows.

Inside were cushioned benches. I counted seven cars on the tram to my left. The lead car had no windows or seats, but an opening to step inside where control monitors lined the front.

We stopped where cables plugged into a control box on the ledge beside the tracks. In front of the lead cars, the tracks turned, extending into an underground tunnel leading outward beyond a barred gate. An identical gate at the inner wall opposed it.

"This goes beneath the city," Ike said, pointing to the inner gate. "We've broken into the sewers through there. This other one goes on forever – the underground tramway. No telling where it leads."

"Can't you charge these trams?" I asked him. "That must be the power box there." I pointed to the control unit. Ike shook his head.

"These solar chargers don't have nearly enough kick," he said. "There's a battery engine in each lead car. This box charges all seven engines."

The charge that brought us down the lift had faded when we returned. Ike gave it another zap so we could get back up. When we reached the room with the map, Hodge was typing on a 'Link device hooked to her ThinkCap. She held a hand up to us, switching off the 'Link once she finished typing.

"That was Lu Calhoun, a friend of the fam. He had a great idea. You know that Tom Hurst guy, the Bio-tech scientist?" The others nodded. It did sound familiar.

"The one who designed those household droids?" asked Deacon.

"He posted text files on the CyberNet about that Kepris outbreak," I remembered. "E-Streams Extracted."

"Right," she confirmed. "Lu lives in Gallagher Heights by Hurst's estate. He'll sneak us up there tomorrow night. By us I mean you and Deacon Blue here. I'll be laying low. Deacon says you can crash at his place." I looked at Deacon; we both looked at Hodge.

"Not trying to impose," I said.

"He doesn't mind," said Hodge. "He owes me. That kid of his could have got us burned today. Thank God it was you, Black."

Deacon smiled and put his hand on my shoulder. "Let's go, compadre."

We climbed the twisted cords up to the gap. The old guy was in shape. He made it to the top without hassle. I followed him, prying my way from the hole near the surface and into the chilling rain again. I followed Deacon past brick units to the one at the end of the vendors' section. Green ivy streaked up the wall that faced us. We walked two stairs to the electric door where Deacon keyed his lock code.

Inside, he flipped a switch, and tube lights glowed on the ceiling. A flowerpot of Easter lilies sat on a white plastic table between two wooden chairs. Plastic shelves along the left wall held a few large pots and pans above the tiny stove. A suede curtain covered a small entranceway at the back, and a ladder beside it reached a hatch in the ceiling.

Deacon lifted the lid from an old trunk near the door, retrieving a long-necked white bottle and two tin cups. He unscrewed the cap and poured two drinks.

"My daughter Naudica sleeps on the cot in the back," he said, handing me a cup. "The floor isn't bad."

I expected wine for some reason, and the sting of strong liquor almost choked me. There was a bittersweet aftertaste. Deacon chuckled, patting my back hard as I coughed.

"That's the White Lightning," he said. Handing me the bottle, he closed the chest and climbed the ladder at the back wall, balancing his cup on the top rung. He opened a pad lock and flipped the hatch with his free hand, motioning for me to follow.

I climbed onto the uneven roof where Deacon sat at the edge beside Augie, the wolf from earlier, who'd climbed up from outside. I sat beside them, placed the bottle between us and gazed toward the city. Screens and holos displayed ads everywhere. Some flashed so quickly I couldn't decipher meaning. One screen near the top of a building far off read, "Purchase Network® Shares." A list of Net links rolled up the screen like the prologue to Star Wars, except it said things like, "www.ak19002."

"If you look at those too long, they'll program your thought patterns," Deacon said. "Neurotechs have it to an exact science – images and light, something like DeLillo's 'waves and radiation.'"

I dug into my jacket for the plastic-wrapped cigars. Two left. I took one out to light.

"Wouldn't have an extra, would you?" he asked.

"Sure," I reached for the other cigar. "Last one."

I lit it for him. He puffed deep and exhaled a cloud, looking again toward the city. A weight in the air seemed lifted. Augie curled his tail and rested his huge head on his paws. His wintery eyes were half open, watching the screens with disinterest.

"We're leaving this place, friend," Deacon said, "Once this thing with Hodge blows over."

"Leaving the city?" I asked. He nodded, blowing smoke.

"Who knows what we'll find on the outside. Might find a warp gate to the heavens." He looked at me. "Naudica's not allowed off this wall. They say she has some kind of mutation. I'm the reason we're even up here."

"How?" I wondered.

"Preaching the good news," he answered. "You familiar?"

The question caught me off guard. "Never imagined people in different worlds could share beliefs," I said.

"You a believer then?" he asked.

"It's hard to wrap my head around," I admitted. "Everything seems out of context." Deacon nodded slowly as I took another long puff.

"It's not easy to believe in anything," he said, squinting at the cigar he held between a thumb and two fingers. "Even my wife lost faith, like Job's wife." After a pause, he faced me, taking another puff. "What will you do, friend?" Screens on the nearest building stopped running ads momentarily, flashing a sequence of orange and blue.

Frame a famous Biotech scientist, I thought. It was another job I'd pull for Hodge. Lead Eye was with me for the first. We'd gotten tickets to an election assembly for the new Citizen Rep in East Two-O' Nine to expose the face of a candidate known as Big Woody, whom both Hodge and Lead Eye swore was a robot. I had my doubts when I saw him at the bench with the other candidates, looking perfectly human. I'd distracted the crowd, collapsing on the floor and convulsing like I'd had a meltdown, as was the plan. Hodge slipped through the crowd and shot Big Woody through the ear multiple times. Lead Eye jumped down to the bench, gripped Woody around the jaws with his robot hand and ripped his face right off.

They were right, it turned out. Shrieks of fear turned to shocked gasps when people saw wiring behind the face of a man most in the district favored to represent them in the GenPub assembly.

But that seemed small time compared to this. Nahzir's Regime rarely intervened in public affairs but was sure to show up when scientific research was involved, and Tom Hurst was the top guy in his field.

Still, Hodge took me in like a guardian. She'd given me gear, food, a badge to walk the streets. She was just an army surplus junkie, but the public saw her as a criminal. She wasn't so bad – a little pushy, but just a misfit like me. So was Lead Eye.

They were on my side, if there was a side to be on. And this guy Deacon had sincerity in his voice, a glint of hope in his eyes, that rare sort of optimistic hope for the good in mankind that makes you want to keep on believing.

I flexed the fist of my newly forming hand, feeling more strength than before. The muscle and bone seemed sturdier.

"A warp gate to heaven?" I said.

"Right," said Deacon, refilling his empty glass. He took a drink, staring contentedly toward the city. "Just one last job." I could almost feel his hope, like energy emanating from him.

E-Streams Extracted
Log-004..

    I slid two ten-byte tokens into the Stargazer's rusty frame under a faded number seven. They clacked along the inner workings. A tray popped out with a visor headset. I strapped it on, and the world around me turned hazy. Sapphire clouds drifted lazily over cloudscrapers and iridescent holos along the skyline above Gallagher Heights.

    Orange sprites appeared, etching details that slowly took form to create the perfect face – Anna's face. The Stargazer's eyes glowed. It spoke inside my head, telling me I'd lost something precious in the recent past and could possibly lose something else just as valuable. Before the image flickered out, it said a cliché about staying the path to find what I seek.

    I can't remember the voice. Maybe there wasn't one. The head unit was warm, and I felt the heat flowing through me. Don't know if the sensation was real or just brain signals, but I think my soul's been touched.......

Thomas Hurst -- NewStream Daily

Chapter 5

Deacon eyed the radar map on the dash as we raced through the sewers. The battery cart had some thrust to it. I gripped the side rail as Deacon swerved through tunnels. "Staying off paths with lots of heat signals," he said, pointing to the GPS screen beside the wheel. Our white beacon approached a red dot ahead. Clusters of red dots drifted in areas further out on the map.

"Guards?" I asked. He shook his head.

"ID drones. Heavily armed. They guard something below these sewers." I thought of Ike's theory, imagining a massive mother generator kilometers below us with thousands of Omega beams branching from it.

We spotted the drone in front of a raised floodgate. Deacon saw it too, a swivel gun mounted on four rubber wheels, rolling through puddles from yesterday's rain. A coiled neck on top of the gun turned a glass eye toward us.

"Take the wheel," Deacon directed, standing in his seat and reaching for the burner slung over his back. I tried to hold steady, tipping the wheel to and fro. Bullets rattled, sparking the drone's neck. Its gun swiveled on us as we whizzed by. Deacon spun in the seat, peeked through his scope and cracked off more rounds. Something exploded in the side mirror, closer than it appeared. Sparks blazed from the droid's shattered eye as it fired blindly at the sewer wall. I slid to the driver's seat as Deacon climbed in the back.

"Take the left path there." He pointed at two narrow tunnels ahead. The left sloped up; the right one took a sharp, downward curve. I raised my thumb off the accelerator and steered up the slope to a wide, level area with a low ceiling. Drain covers stretched the top of the right wall every ten yards or so, as far down as I could see. Wind blew in as cart tires rumbled past the drain covers, rattling ones with loose screws.

"Stop here," Deacon said. "That green button on the wheel's the brake. Don't press hard, just tap it." I did, easing to a stop. Deacon flipped the off switch behind the wheel and climbed a ladder at the corner wall by the nearest drain cover. It led to a tunnel between buildings above the street. Squeezing through the narrow tunnel, we edged through vertical iron bars onto an upper terrace of stylish stone condos. Light shined at the edges of curtained windows and balcony doors on identical condos across a dead-end alley of gray shadows.

The alley opened to the street we'd seen through the storm drains below, where eight-lane traffic passed both ways.

"This is University Way," said Deacon as we stepped from the alley. Commuter carts were parked bumper to bumper along the curb. The neon-lit street was alive with city walkers. Several blocks away, a vast dish-shaped platform was nested between three cloudscrapers. Tall trees poked above the edge of the dish. Beneath it, immense steel columns riveted the platform to the structures around it. Bright letters at its curved base flashed, "Gallagher Heights."

"Lu lives in those heights," Deacon pointed. "He'll show us to Hurst's place."

Nearing the intersection at Kohl Road, Gallagher Heights was directly above us. The South Eight StreetTram bowled along a caged track above the median, racing the eastbound traffic. A glass elevator shaft extended from the roof of a one-story glass building at the corner to the underside of the metallic disk stories above. Further down the street, an orange cart pulled into the entrance of a parking bay that stretched the length of the block.

"We'll make a stop first," said Deacon. We crossed Kohl as the signal stopped the traffic and stepped into Hal's Spirits on the ground floor of the East Gallagher tower. The tall shelves in the store looked like bookcases. Wide bottles with elegant caps sat on the shelves facing the checkout counter. A man stood behind the counter with a pearly white smile stuck to his face.

"Welcome to Hal's," he beamed. I nodded as we walked past. Deacon ignored him. His unblinking eyes followed us to the coolers along the far wall facing the entrance. His smile was still frozen. I shrugged it off and followed Deacon past the coolers stacked with ales of arbitrary flavors like, "Golden Fields" and "Moonlit Harvest," to the back of the store. These shelves held large unlabeled bottles. I recognized the long-necked white ones on the middle shelf. They were identical to the one Deacon and I drank last night.

He handed me two bottles and we cut through the center aisle to the front, passing packets of trail mix, candy and dried fruit, dehydrated garlic rolls and spinach wraps in tidy, flat boxes that said "Just soak in water and serve." At the end were Mars candy bars and colorful plastic cups. We stood at the checkout. The weirdo clerk was still smiling, making me uneasy.

"Two-point-six kils, please," he said through his smile, looking at me. Deacon held up a red currency card. The smiling man scanned it and hastily bagged the items.

We left the store, stood at the curb and waited to cross the street.

"The hell was wrong with that guy?" I asked Deacon.

He looked at me. "That was a replica. Can't you tell people from robots?"

I said, "Apparently not." Deacon laughed as the signal changed and we stepped off the curb.

"Neither can I," he said.

We entered the tinted building across the street, the "Heights Security Office," as the door sign read. A security guard sat behind a tall desk across from two lounge chairs, eyeing us with interest – or suspicion. I gave him a friendly nod, and Deacon pressed "9 8 1" on a numbered wall panel between two small, potted trees in ceramic pots. A beep sounded from the speaker, and a man's voice said, "Be right down."

We stood at the panel, watching the bronze elevator across the office. After long awkward silence, the door opened, and a tan-brown man in expensive looking shades stepped off. He had a thin-shaved mustache and sideburns, and somehow looked familiar.

"Hey," he said grinning. "Brought the real stuff, yah? Parade's just starting." We followed Lu onto the lift. He shook Deacon's hand, then mine. He wore a high-tech 'Link device on his arm – a spiked gauntlet with a touch screen.

"I hear Hodge pissed off the Regime. I told her I'd do what I could. She's loyal fam." He tilted his head, cracking bones in his neck. Swift clouds scurried across the pearl half moon between cloudscrapers as we shot above the busy street. In moments, the vastness of Starlight City stretched all around us. An instant later, we entered the dish and the colorful world disappeared.

The doors opened. We walked a dirt path between flat-trimmed bushes. The path ended at a cobblestone walk that snaked through lush grass, stopping at the sandy edge of a canal that curved along the heights.

Lights along a wooden bridge crossing the canal shone on the crystal-clear water, which reflected holos on cloudscrapers and the starlight above with picture clarity. I heard a splash and looked below. A goldfish swam through the lights, skimming white pebbles at the bottom.

Flowers grew along the opposite bank where the stone path led to the neighborhood of lavish estates with one and two-story homes. They all had rounded walls, and Acacia trees dotted the grass around them. The nearest home sat far back from the walk.

Lu crossed the lawn of the second house to a wide porch framed by oak trees. Happy folks were crowded on the porch, most holding wine glasses or mugs with foaming ale. Two men wearing similar jackets with flipped collars sat at a glass table in canvas chairs by the porch, playing cards with a woman in pencil-thin pink shades.

"We can talk inside," Lu said. We headed through the door into the front room. More people crowded on conjoined sofas, intently watching six gamers with visors and laser guns shoot at holographic soldiers on the wall screen.

The marble hallway curved under winding stairs and ended at an empty guest room. Lu shut the door behind us. The room had a rounded shape, and a cozy-looking bed hung from the wall between two tall aquariums where tiny florescent fish swam lazy circles.

"I checked Hurst's spot when I got off the 'Link with Hodge," Lu said. "Somebody decoded the door. It was open. Hurst's neighbor, Saul, says the guy hasn't been there in five cycles. Works for the Regime."

"What's the house number?" asked Deacon.

"Just stick to the walk," he said. "Once you pass the Commonwealth Center, his estate will be on the right."

We left the house, continuing along the stone path, passing two homes beside Lu's, similar in size and design. Soon, we approached a large bust of a bird-nosed man beside a path branching to paved steps of the Commonwealth Center. A granite plaque in the grass read "Kato The Architect."

Headlights beamed from an air cart flying overhead. I froze as it tilted our way. Deacon nudged me forward. "Just a rental," he said. The cart passed over us and descended behind the center.

At Hurst's place, an old willow tree stood to one side of the porch steps. The windows were dark. On the porch, an old wooden swing with clouds on the cushions hung motionless, as if suspended in time.

We pushed through the unlocked door, stepping into a front room much like Lu's. Crystal lamps sat on four glass tables, casting a dim glow over still photographs. In the hallway, a digitally rendered horizon met violet clouds and deep blue sky over a snowy countryside. The framed landscape was mounted beside the entrance to Hurst's island kitchen, where a diamond clock on the stove shined "27:04" through the dark.

Deacon opened a door beneath the stairway. Lights flickered as we crept down carpeted stairs into a wash area. Empty metal bins and glass containers were stacked across four large sinks.

"Hurst's lab," said Deacon.

The middle section of the lab was disorderly. Papers lay scattered across a round, metal desk with a StarMack projector mounted over a hole in the center. A pale, rubber face with a white beard lying at the edge of the desk seemed oddly out of place. Cords connected it to a box that resembled an antique television. Un-insulated wires from the box hung through the hole beneath the StarMack projector, attaching to a magnetic Omega power strip on the floor.

The round navigator orb on the curved keypad glowed white as we approached.

"Might find something on his StarMack," Deacon said. He sat in the rolling chair and nudged his fingers against the orb.

Multicolor holo icons spawned above the table. A comet sprite lit the icons as Deacon skimmed through them. I watched his fingers press the rolling orb softly to lower the sprite pointer; pinching his fingertips against it raised it slightly.

Walking to the back wall, I slid open one of several large white cabinets. My heartbeat spiked when I saw what was inside. Leaping back, I tripped and fell over a trash bin.

"What is it?" Deacon shined his rifle flashlight into the open cabinet. The replica was so lifelike, and beautiful. I'd seen the face before; I remembered – the mission in space, in my old life, scouting an alien spacecraft. The nightmare had actually happened.

"Black, what's the matter?"

"I've seen this before." My heart kept pounding.

"That's one of Hurst's household droids, I think," Deacon said. "He designed the prototypes. Neo University sold the designs to some corporation. My mother had one. You just synch it to your StarMack and download functions.

I sat there, afraid to move.

"I'll show you," he said, standing from the chair. "I'm sure Hurst has functions on here for it." He pulled the replica from the cabinet on a rolling apparatus, wheeling it over to the StarMack.

"Maybe not a good idea," I said.

"Hurst hasn't been here in five cycles," he assured me.

"But the door was unlocked," I protested, though I wasn't afraid of someone showing up. I was afraid of the replica. Deacon sat down again, moving the sprite to activate a "Functions" icon. The other icons vanished, and a file cabinet appeared. He leafed through a list of smaller icons in a folder labeled "Recent downloads" and stopped at a pulsing icon of a silver tree growing from a colorful planet I recognized as Earth.

"Here's an Alpha code encryption," he said. "Alpha's the one my mom's used. Let's see what functions Hurst planned to download." He clicked on the icon. A transparent blue cube labeled *Dreams Deterred* superimposed the folder's contents.

There were undecipherable characters in the cube. Deacon dragged at a scrollbar. It barely moved, but countless lines of text raced up the screen. A caption below the cube said, "Decoding aborted."

"What sort of function is this?" he wondered. "Maybe we've found something. Let's plug her in."

"I'm not so sure," I said, my mind racing backwards. I knew I was from Earth, but until that moment, I couldn't remember how I'd ended up on Neon. Now the nightmare flooded back – my first and last mission as a Harmonica Soldier of Peace, the stealth pod flight from Lunar Six to the foreign spacecraft – the childish laughter of the beautiful monster that killed us.

Deacon lifted the black hair hanging down the replica's back. "The data chip's usually in the neck, I think." He found a loose panel of the fair skin and peeled it back like tape, exposing tiny slots on the metal frame beneath.

A strange voice said, "The fug are you doing down here?"

We spun around. A guy stood at the foot of the stairs, his army flack torn in several places. "NeoRegime" was sewn on the collar. He gave a cold stare from forest-green eyes that glowed like holos.

Deacon raised his burner. I saw a blue spark, and the guy cleared about twenty-five feet between him and us. A white flash snapped Deacon's burner in half before he could aim. The guy hurled Deacon across the room; he slammed against the cabinet and hit the floor unconscious. In the next tick, I was tacked to the adjacent wall and my shades flew off. The guy held me off the floor, pressing against my chest.

"Who are you?" His voice was artificial, like it came from a speaker.

"Me? I'm nobody," I choked out.

"So am I," he said. "What are you doing in my dad's lab?" I tried to speak, but the pressure from his arm constricted my air. He released me and I collapsed to a knee, catching my breath.

"Your dad..." I coughed out. "Hurst?"

"I know you." He peered into my face. "The Rebirth specimen."

This is it, I thought. The end of my run. "I'm not going back to wherever you psychos put me back together," I said. "You'll have to kill me right here."

"Never enjoyed the killing," he said, offering a hand to help me up. "It was me who cut you loose. I saw what happened to the other two soldiers they found on that ship. That wasn't right."

Other two soldiers? My mind raced. How many of us were there? Was I the only one still alive? Trying to recall details brought only blurred moments to mind of me drifting in a cold, glowing liquid behind glass, breathing through something stuck down my throat. That was before I woke up on a lab floor with broken glass all around. The door was unlocked, so I ran for dear life.

Deacon was coming to again. I went to help him stand.

"What in God's...?" He rubbed the back of his head.

"Had some collision there," I said. Deacon tensed when he saw the soldier staring at the replica of the woman, touching its face.

"You haven't told me why you're here," the guy said without looking at us. "This is my dad's house. You can't steal anything."

"Your dad?" Deacon said. "That's – you're Griffin Hurst?"

"Griffin Hurst died," he said, turning to us. "I'm just Griff."

"Hurst never found a cure?" asked Deacon, seemingly surprised. "They said he was transferred to the some military site, I assumed to work on the Kepris cure."

"He found something Nahzir thought was better; a way to transfer conscious data. Now he's a puppet. I need to set him free."

"But you're alive. He must have cured you."

Griff held up his right arm, which snapped open at the elbow. A jagged blade extended from a shiny robotic limb.

"This isn't Griffin's body."

"A machine," I said, bewildered. "You're inside a machine?"

"A murder weapon," he replied. There was something in his glowing eyes unmistakably human – like disgust. "You didn't answer my question," he demanded. Deacon and I exchanged a nervous glance.

"We..." Deacon scratched his partially graying head.

"We were trying to frame Hurst," I finished. Lying was probably a bad idea.

"Our friend Hodge was wrongly accused of a crime," Deacon added. "The terrorist attack at the university. We're trying to clear her name. And Hurst has ties to the university, so we thought..." He trailed off.

"A logical approach," I added, hoping the guy could relate. "We don't have a vendetta against him. I've never met the man."

"You're wasting your time," Griff said. "Nahzir needed an excuse to oversee neurology research at the university. People believe everything on those holos."

"They framed Hodge?" Deacon asked. "Why? She runs a bar and a gadget shop."

"She sells weapons, right? Beverly Hodge?" said Griff. "A logical scapegoat."

Griff decided he was coming with us, and neither of us objected. He stood on the cobblestone walk facing dark clouds of a front approaching from the East when Deacon and I brought Lu out to see him.

"You're that alpha human," said Lu, containing surprise. "I know a couple nut jobs trying to claim that eighty-gig reward Nahzir put up for you."

"What about you?" Griff asked, still gazing up. Lu held his hands up defensively.

"I don't do it for the bytes," he answered. "Got my own reasons to hunt." Griff was silent. He looked at Lu. The anger I'd seen in his eyes was gone. He seemed to have emerged from a daydream.

"You guys can probably get out of here unnoticed," Lu said, "But you can't stroll around in that tattered uniform. The streets have eyes."

E-Streams Extracted
Log-005..

Two cycles ago, after Anna died, I started plans for a new kind of cyborg. We called it Project Anna II and designed the prototype in her image as my way of honoring her. She was my light, even though I hardly told her – but I'm sure she knew.

My colleagues showed support then. I'd hoped the prototype could lead us to information about the disease that claimed Anna's life. But several science gurus on NewStream Daily posted comments on the project, portraying me as some heartsick maniac, even suggested I was secretly creating a sex cyborg that looked like Anna. Regime officials showed up at the collegiate doors and ordered us to abort the project. It mattered naught that the cyborg was a breakthrough in Biotech research – a humanoid that could gather data from regions of the Forests where microorganisms are too deadly for even a quasi-human to survive.

The new prototype sits on a sliding stand in the big storage cabinet here in my basement. I'll finish the work alone once we figure out how to control this virus; screw the Regime. They'll know once they see the innovation. I'll make them pay attention.

The only thing she needs now is a program for the CyberNet® brain that will run her. We used the human brain as a base model for the cerebral functions. I wonder how that Stargazer© was programmed. No one is fascinated by them anymore, but the coding seems ingenious, if you really consider it. There's something mystical about it. *I bet it's still in the neighborhood...* Ah, thinking out loud now.......

Thomas Hurst -- NewStream Daily

Chapter 6

We followed Lu around his house to a patio deck overlooking an in-ground pool. Behind trees at the back of the lawn, dim lights streamed the top edge of the height's platform disk.

A lovely, brown-eyed woman with copper hair and brown freckles sat alone in an umbrella chair beside the pool, holding a tall wine glass. Stairs behind her led to a patio door with drapes half drawn.

The woman paused between sips, looking at Griff, then glanced wide-eyed at Lu.

"Friends of mine," Lu grinned at her. "This is Melia." We nodded. She forced a half smile that somehow conveyed the words, "Are you serious?"

"My pleasure," said Deacon with a grin.

Lu took us through a door at the end of the patio deck into a rec room with three billiard tables. Another door led to a carpeted basement with electronic weight machines and a punching bag in the near corner. He typed on a button panel next to the stairs. The far wall slid aside to reveal an armory of high-tech firearms.

"Grab a tool in case you need it. Hodge's brother saw some guards searching the wall district. Doesn't sound good."

I found a chrome .45 Colt with a wooden handle.

"Take whatever you find in that closet there," he said to Griff, pointing to a white door in the mirrored back wall. Griff opened it, sliding clothes across the rack. He chose a long, black and gray patterned cloak with a loose hood similar to Deacon's. It was like a trench cloak with a cape flare, a popular style. He zipped it over his uniform.

"Thanks," Griff said, looking at himself in the mirror wall. He pulled the hood down enough to shadow his face.

The lift took us back to the security office where the guard still sat behind the counter. He ignored us now, watching something on a screen.

"Thanks for stopping through," Lu said to us. "And thanks for the booze. Hey, you guys take the tram here? I'll give you a ride."

We stepped into the living street. Lu led us to the parking bay entrance down the block, pausing to touch icons on his 'Link. In moments, a black four-dour cart cruised through the bay door with no driver and parked beside us. Its wide base sat low to the ground between slick, bulky tires. Lu took the wheel while Deacon and I sat in the cramped backseat. Griff rode shotgun.

The interior was like the cockpit of a spaceship, or a high tech fighter jet. The dash was chrome-silver, with plasma screens and indigo dials. One screen on Lu's side displayed weather conditions on a Doppler map; another played news streams.

Lu controlled everything – steering, braking, and acceleration – with a multi-button analog stick at his side. He turned on the sound system, and bass thumped in rhythm to an oddly nostalgic sound. The info screen read *Playlist 7 – Clock With No Hands*.

Lu whipped between cars along the street. The ride was silky smooth.

"We'll split up," said Deacon. "I'm guessing you two aren't cleared for the tram. I'll get back to the Diamond."

"We'll keep a low profile," I told Griff. "I know a spot we can lay low." While Deacon called Hodge on the 'Link, Lu sped through a caution signal as it flashed, *Stop* in red.

"She isn't picking up," said Deacon. "Hope nothing's happened."

Four streets down, Lu cut a sharp right.

"Stay on Southbound," said Deacon. "We'll let them off by South Main station."

"Going south," Lu replied. "I'll take Skyway Seventy-one."

"This is a racing cart?" Deacon looked surprised.

"You can't tell by the tires?" replied Lu. He hung a hard left into aggressive traffic converging onto a ramp that sloped toward the skyline. We passed beneath a Level Three transit interval, crossing overtop the Skye Electronica and Vizio buildings, ascending still higher.

Lu accelerated to a jarring speed, approaching five tunnels ahead. He maneuvered quickly between cars and swerved into the "Southbound" tunnel at the center, blasting the accelerator. The ride was still smooth, but there was a weightless feeling in the pit of my stomach.

Pulling onto exit ramp "S-119" was like slowing for a pit stop. Lu braked hard. The lower half of the sign said "Portside." The ramp curved in wide spirals until it reached the ground and became Harris Road, which Lu took to Seaside View, letting us off at the place I showed him by the shore walk.

"I'll check on Hodge," said Deacon as I stepped out. "Take this." He removed a gold chain with a "fishers of men" symbol from around his neck. "That's my 'Link device. I'll call you when I find Hodge."

I shut the door, and Lu peeled off.

Griff and I slipped over the shore walk rail onto the sea wall. The pearl moon lit ghostly cloud plumes on a horizon of endless sea. Two sailboats with neon hull lights coasted toward the dock.

Seagulls perched on the iron drainpipes cawed as Griff followed me across. The gulls scattered as the pipes quivered beneath Griff's feet. He must have had an entire frame of steel.

We entered the sewer near the dock, beneath the street. Passing beneath the Café Shack, I could see the abstract graffiti ahead but not the pale light. When we reached the bend, broken chains of Lead Eye's makeshift gate hung to the ground.

"Split in half," I said. "Someone came after him."

"Friend of yours?" asked Griff. I nodded.

In the small living space, there was a box sitting on the Rubbermaid tote. Its plastic seal was broken, and inside were unopened packs of fresh cigars. I stuffed a few in my vest.

"Maybe they found him," I pondered.

"Now what?" asked Griff.

"Hopefully he went to the Diamond."

We took an AutoBus out to the west end. I wondered what contraptions Griff would use to climb the steel wall, but he didn't climb. He moon jumped right on top of it, at least twenty stories high. A white halo of smoke rose from where he'd stood beside me.

When I climbed up to meet him, there seemed to be a lot more residents roaming about, though it was still pretty late. The rain last time must have kept most folks inside. A group of hooded youngsters stood laughing and joking loudly by a space heater where Griff waited. I led him through the crowded vendors' section and past Deacon's unit to the gap in the wall. We both crawled inside.

Hodge was there with Deacon, whose head was lowered like when I first saw him. A news stream showing Hodge's picture played on the wall, and a holo newswoman stood beside it, speaking to the camera.

"Deacon said you'd have a guest," Hodge said, looking at Griff. "The fugitive alpha human in the flesh." She smiled. "Where's Lead Eye?"

"Someone broke into his spot," I answered. "Hoped he'd be here."

"More bad news? Guards are roaming around. They might have tracked my 'Link transmissions. Can't use it anymore."

Griff approached the door next to the newswoman. "What is this place?" he asked.

"An armory," Hodge answered.

"How could – " Griff's hand snapped open. He sliced the lock with a blade in his wrist and slid the electronic door, which creaked and groaned from rust. He walked to the edge of the balcony and looked around.

"An armory inside the wall."

"That's what I said," Hodge repeated, stepping out to join him. I followed them. Griff looked along the ceiling some distance to the right, where a large rusted swivel gun faced away from us. I hadn't noticed it before.

"Someone put hella machine power into building all this," Hodge added. She hung on her last word as Griff jumped the guardrail, free-falling multiple stories to the bottom, hitting the ground with a loud bang. We rushed to the edge and looked down.

He was the size of my thumb from so high, walking among the battery carts. "That was unexpected," Hodge uttered in quiet shock.

Hodge used her penlight's solar charger to power the lift as we stepped on.

"Where's Deacon?" I wondered, looking back through the gate.

"Thanking God for getting us through the day," Hodge replied.

On the ground, we rode a cart to where Griff stood in front of the old tram system, looking at the barred gate of the underground tramway Ike had shown me.

"We should see where this leads," Griff said as we hopped out

"I've driven a cart in there as far as it'll go," said Hodge. "These solar chargers only last so many revs without real sunlight. I'm trying to make an Omega engine for one. Then I could drive all the way through, if there is an end."

"You used that generator near the lift to design your engine," Griff said. Hodge glanced at me.

"How'd you know that?"

"Logical deduction," Griff replied. "I want to see it. Ancient architects must have built it."

We all squeezed inside the generator. Griff examined the iron wheel.

"These aren't like Nahzir's," he said. "They're primitive, which makes them more complex, mathematically. There's no vacuum for resistance."

"I tried to get this one to move around. There's too much rust on the wheel."

"The magnets lost power from wear. Once a generator is activated, it functions indefinitely. Whoever built this had it turned off."

"So we know for sure the Regime didn't build it," said Hodge. "It was a past civilization."

"The Life Bomb wiped them out is my guess. Nahzir claims his father discovered this planet." Griff narrowed his glowing eyes, and a chill must have rushed through me.

"Life bomb?" said Hodge. "How can you be sure?"

Griff had already stepped outside.

We followed him toward the trams. Hodge seemed lost in thought as she studied the ground. She looked ahead toward Griff.

"The Life Bomb created spontaneous life on Neon," Hodge said. "It didn't destroy it. I've done my research."

"Maybe you don't fully understand life," Griff said as he kept walking. "Life feeds on life. Species created by a Life Bomb rapidly evolve with the atmosphere the explosion creates. Because of the hyper-aggressive HeLa cells Nahzir's father modified, any combination of gene strands in the bomb can fuse, which creates all kinds of volatile microorganisms and mutants. I'm sure the famous chimera hunter could tell you about the Forests on Neon."

He nodded at Lu, then walked between us to the tram control box. He reached inside it, pulling coils of dusty, insulated wires. Sparks popped loudly in his hand, and electricity surged through the tracks. Lights inside tramcars slowly flickered on, illuminating dust clouds swirling above the seat cushions.

"Heaven's holiday," whispered Hodge.

"We can use this place as a stronghold," said Griff.

"For what?" I asked.

"To fight the Regime."

"You out of your mind?" Hodge laughed.

"There's plenty of artillery here. Recruit residents and train them. I can charge those generator magnets."

"Why would we fight the Regime?" asked Hodge. "We just want to get out of here."

"Then get out while you can," Griff said. "They'll find this place soon. I'm here to kill Nahzir either way. I need to set my dad free – and I need to see Jada."

"Who?" Hodge wondered.

"She's alpha human like me," he said, stopping near the tram on the center track. "She's all I've thought of these five cycles I've been gone. I can't figure out why." He climbed into the tram control car. I saw him pressing buttons on the console. Hodge flipped a remote lever on the control box that lifted the bars of the outward gate.

"I'm going down this tunnel," Griff said, still fiddling with the console inside. The tram's wheels screeched as they pulled a few yards along the track and stopped. Hodge stepped inside with him.

"This is it, kids," Hodge said. "You coming, Black?"

I started for the stair, then, paused.

"I should find Lead Eye," I told her. "Check a few more spots."

"You're right," she returned with a nod. "I'll have Ike take you

his ex-wife's place. Let's all meet back here."
 The old tram rattled into the tunnel and was gone

E-Streams Extracted
Log-006..

I might be in some trouble. Not sure if I'm thinking clearly – or maybe I'm seeing clearer than ever. I took my micro saw set and stalked that Stargazer© down after dusk, luring it behind the Commonwealth Center by the rental air carts parked in the lot. I sabotaged it, stripping it down and dragging the headpiece and other components with it, sticking to shadows on my way back to the pad. The scraps are sitting on my desk. The engineer used the standard Genesis model for the robotics, with some modifications to the scheme. I need to study the modifications and figure out what makes this thing work. The Kepris anticode can wait. There's something here I haven't considered before.......

Thomas Hurst -- NewStream Daily

Chapter 7

People thought the wall district was odd. West Four-Eighteen was even stranger. Starlight City ran on citizen law enforcement, but some districts upheld certain laws less than others.

"Organized crime thrives there," Ike said. He stood above me at the end of the crowded tram platform in the wall district. The West-17 tram curved around a cloudscraper where Ike pointed, racing beneath the sloped track. "Most people turn the other way if they see something they ain't supposed to." He was pointing the apartment building out to me, where "Twenty-two E" was spelled down the top corner. I still didn't have a badge, so I'd need to find a way to meet Ike there in thirty spins.

"You've been to the Riff Raff Tav' before," he said. "It's not far from there."

I remembered the first time I met Hodge at the Tav'…

*   *   *

I'd stepped off the AutoBus with Lead Eye on Center Street. At ground level was an industrial park with vast buildings beneath Macroware Plaza.

Most of the city walkers there were robots. Some wheeled in and out of buildings where other bots on the inside made products from polymer plastics. Steel products were made in glass compounds with fuming smokestacks. Commuter carts and other products were built in these factories.

Some of the bots could only be described as walking televisions, some with blank, blue flat-screens; others had wire antennas with static noise. As Lead Eye led me toward the Zahncorp Pharmaceutics factories, several of these walking screens followed us around, constantly watching us.

We'd taken a lift in the Macroware building up to the plaza. The Riff Raff Tav' was across the platform.

There were a few late afternoon drinkers inside. Lead Eye had landed himself in the nearest seat at the bar where Hodge and another woman served drinks. Hodge glanced at Lead Eye, then looked me up and down.

"You're Black, eh?" she'd asked. "Funny name. I'm Hodge. Got work for you if you're interested." I nodded. She slid a drink to a man in a black leather cap watching a bar top holo of two armor-clad warriors fighting with swords. She handed a slip to the other bartender.

"The guy on the end has a steak on the grill." Hodge had pointed to a heavyset man on the opposite side. "Don't let it get tough. I'll be back in a spin." The girl nodded, and Hodge took us through a door behind the bar to a back room. Another door opened to a dark hallway. She keyed in a door down the hall, and lights flickered on as we entered. On shelves all around were high-tech toys and action figures. There were mechanical pets, radio-controlled cars, helicopters and several planes, all different sizes.

"My gadget shop," she said.

Dozens of antique computer parts and circuit boards with exposed wires lay on display tables. In a corner near the customer entrance was a model of Starlight City.

"I build these gadgets by hand with a few air tools and a micro saw set. That's the workstation." She pointed to an odd StarMack interface in the opposite corner. The projector hung in front of the seat from a curved stand overhead. Beneath it was a wide shelf with slots holding various tools. I was more fascinated by the model city, which sat on a large glass base. There didn't seem to be one detail missed, from street signs to building screens. She couldn't have built this entire thing by hand, I'd thought. Starlight City was massive, a metropolis nearly twenty miles long from the southern sea port to the northern tip of the Diamond.

"You like that?" she had asked, walking over to it. She clicked a black button on the base and the model flared with color.

Screens lit up, and tiny holos appeared.

"That's impossible," I said.

"Then this city is impossible," she'd replied. "But it can't be, cause we're standing in it, aren't we?" All I could do was stare at the masterpiece.

"Don't get me wrong," she said. "It's taken over thirty cycles to build this thing. When I was a younger woman, I wanted to be an architect. I studied Kato, the man Nahzir's father hired to design Starlight City. Started building this and just never stopped."

Sitting at her workstation, she'd grabbed a small machine plugged into the interface and took a picture ID card from the shelf. "You can print anything you want over these. All I do is reprogram the barcodes. ID drones can't tell the difference. If someone asks to see it, though, you're in a rut. But who knows. Some can't tell a real from a fake."

*   *   *

This time on my way through West Four-Eighteen, I made sure to avoid those creepy, stalker TVs, taking the long way around the industrial park to the Macroware building. At Level Three, I cut through the plaza, passed the Tav' and headed to the residential area of the district. Ike was waiting in front of building Twenty-two E. People loitered in front of the building, talking excitedly. Inside, red caution tape crossed the stairs leading up. We didn't see a guard around, so we stepped over the tape and started up. A boy stood at the top wearing a yellow poncho and grubby white sneakers.

"Somebody died right there," he said. "I saw him die." I stopped.

"Sorry." I stepped aside awkwardly, avoiding the invisible man. "You knew him?"

"My brother Quinn owed him money. He was going to kill Quinn tomorrow if he didn't pay."

"Your brother's lucky, then," said Ike.

"We're looking for a guy," I said. "Dark skin, long dreads, around my height."

"What kind of guy?" he asked. I should have expected the question.

"A quasi-guy, sort of. Has a metal arm and a robot eye."

"That's Miles's dad. They took him. The one's who killed that flesh guy."

"Who were they?" I asked the boy. He shrugged.

"Miles says they're alpha humans. That's what his dad told him."

"Miles is upstairs?" The boy nodded.

He led us up two floors and knocked on a door by the stairs.

"Quinn, it's me. Quinn, open the door." He knocked until a wiry, shirtless man appeared through a crack in the door with a cig hanging from his lip.

"The fug is this now?" he asked, looking at us.

"They want to see Miles," the boy said. Quinn blew puffs of smoke before stepping aside to let us in. Miles, wearing a black rubber raincoat with a gray hood, stared out the barred window across the unfurnished living room with his back to us.

"Will you tell this kid his mom's dead?" said Quinn. "Call cremation services – or an organ dealer. It's been two days already." I ignored him and crossed the room.

"Miles?" I said. He was silent. "We're friends of your dad. Do you know where they took him?"

"The Zenith," he answered, still facing the window, as if talking to someone outside.

"The hell's that?" Ike asked, looking at me.

"A star base." Miles said.

"Hey," Quinn complained. "You can't stay here. I've got people coming by to do business."

"Yeah, fine," I said, holding up a hand. "Miles, can you help us?"

"I'm not leaving mom," Miles said.

"Come on, Miles. I don't think your mom's with us anymore," said Ike.

"She's not dead," Miles said loudly, turning to face us. He was a shade darker than Lead Eye, but his eyes were clear blue. "Dad got fixed. Why can't they fix mom?"

"They didn't fix your dad," said Quinn. "He's a bleeding robot."

Gripped with anger, I punched Quinn in the gut, shoved him to the wall and held him there, pointing the .45 at him.

"You should close that hole under your nose," I said, glaring at him. Couldn't he see the kid was falling apart? Quinn just stared back.

"Those are some cheap ass shades," he said. "Why don't you take your friends and get out. We don't like snakes around here. I know a snake when I see one."

I almost gave him something worse than a shot to the gut, but Ike grabbed my shoulder. "Dry off, Black," he said. I released Quinn with a shove.

"Miles," Ike said. "Why don't we hang with you at your place." With reluctance, Miles stepped toward us. He glanced at his friend, then, followed us out the door.

Walking down three flights, we reached a room at the end of the hall. The door was missing, and a woman lay on the floor in front of the couch, pale and still. There were burns across her temple.

"Lowly sons of..." Ike started.

"Miles, what if we take your mom with us?" I said.

"Really, Black?" said Ike, rubbing his neck. "How in hell do we do that? Carry her onto the tram? People will assume we're stealing her."

"We have to do something."

"Fine, I'll see what Hodge says."

Hodge didn't answer, so he tried Deacon, who told us Lu could help. It turned out Lu could rent an air cart from the Commonwealth Center any time he pleased. Deacon got him on the 'Link for us. He said he'd pick us up. We wrapped the cold woman in fleece threads and bandage tape we found in the hall closet. Didn't know what else to do.

Lu landed us on the wall district in front of Deacon's unit. Naudica stood on the roof beside Augie as we hovered close. He perked up as the cart's thrusters rumbled the ground and set us down with a jerk. Residents stopped to watch as we got off the cart carrying the wrapped woman with us.

Deacon was expecting us. He let us in and closed the door. Naudica climbed down through the hatch, watching from the ladder as we stood around the plastic table. Her black dress was laced with pink and white butterflies. The flowerpot on the table held carnations of the same color.

"I took everything out of the trunk," said Deacon, squeezing between Ike and me to get past. "We'll lay her inside, if it's alright with Miles. She'll be well covered, at least."

Miles nodded.

Carefully, we lay the wrapped woman inside the trunk, placing the lid over her. We all stood in silence.

"Let's bow our heads," Deacon quietly said. "Righteous God, bless this woman's soul. Keep her, oh Lord, so that she might regenerate by some scientific miracle. Those in agreement, say amen."

We echoed. Silence followed.

"So, what now?" asked Ike, stretching his arms toward the low ceiling with a yawn. Lu cracked his neck loudly.

"Hodge and that Griif fellow have been gone a while," Deacon said. "Maybe it's time we went down there. No news on Lead Eye?"

"Seems he's been taken," Ike said. "By some other alpha humans. Maybe he's still alive."

"Let's get down below," I cut in. "Then we'll decide our next move."

"I want to stay here," said Miles. He looked at Deacon.

"Of course," Deacon answered. "Naudica will keep you company. Just keep the door locked. Augie will stay right outside." I stepped outside after Ike. We stopped cold when we saw three guards standing beside Lu's air cart near the fence. Their own patrol cruiser was parked behind his.

"Whose cart is this?" one guard said. "It's not supposed to be up here." I looked at Ike, who looked at me. Lu stepped in front of us.

"Holy..." the guard tapped his partner. "Hey, it's Lu Calhoun."

"Get the," the other started in disbelief, sliding up his visor to get a better look.

"You're a crazy bugger, you know that?" said the first guard.

"Man, don't flatter me, kid," Lu laughed.

"Why didn't you sign up to catch that alpha human?" the guard asked.

"I ain't that crazy," Lu replied. "They say nothing can kill them things."

"Just teasing you, bro. What you doing way out here?"

Lu paused. "I'm, uh. It's funny, actually. I ain't supposed to talk about it, but a research group is paying me to take some humanoids with no military training on my next tour. They want to see if they can survive in the Forests for a week. But I plan to do them one better. I'm recruiting these lowlifes here, and we're gonna catch that prize specimen Nahzir's been after."

It took me a second to realize I was the prize specimen he was talking about. I had a gut feeling they all knew and hadn't said anything.

"That's nuts, man," the second guard replied. "Going out without a real team?" They both looked impressed. Lu shrugged it off.

"Can't wait to see that on your show." They climbed into their cruiser and saluted Lu. He returned the gesture.

"Keep watching," Lu said. The cruiser rose, sailing toward the city.

"We'll be on your show?" Ike smiled cynically at Lu.

"The hell'd you want me to say?" Lu defended. "It was all I could think of."

"You have a show?" I asked him. "A holo show?" The last thing I wanted was to find myself on a reality show. Didn't need the attention.

"Not by choice, believe me," answered Lu. "Once my camerawoman hears I'm up here, she'll hunt me down."

"Word spreads fast over the Net," said Deacon. "Let's hurry down." He turned to Naudica peering halfway out the door.

"Keep the door locked, and don't go on the roof."

"'Kay, Pop." she said. Deacon stepped inside, returning seconds later with a bottle of his White Lightning.

"I'll follow you," said Lu. "Feel like I should get out of sight."

Inside the Diamond, the four of us took an army cart to the tunnel gates. The tram carrying Hodge and Griff was still missing from the center track.

"If Hodge wants to fight, we'll need weapons on hand," Ike said. "Residents will want to join up. I'll bring some crates down the lift."

We spent the next two revs riding up and down the lift, hauling crates of weapons and ammo from upper-level barracks to the tram control station. We placed more crates on the army carts and along the upper balcony.

Then, we waited.

Hodge and Griff wouldn't return until the next day. We smoked cigars and drank White Lightning straight from the bottle until it was empty. Lu told a story about his stint in the military, and about his complicated history with Melia, the woman we saw on his deck by the pool. He talked about the Forests, and his strange experiences out there.

Chapter 8

Lu's Coincidence

◆

I was wired about becoming a NeoPilot that day I enlisted. It was after the Walking Dead Festival, when city walkers all wear masks until sunrise. I walked through East One-Ninety-One to return the wallet of the masked woman I'd slept with the previous night. That was before I'd realized who she was. I bumped into her man Randy in front of the building. He was my best friend. Luckily, I hadn't gone in yet. He told me, "Splice some wigs out there, Lu. Come back in one piece."

I said I would, but never gave much thought to what enlisting actually entailed. It didn't take long to realize I'd stepped into hell.

Training alone was grisly enough at a secret camp in the Argyle Mountains. We were up every morn before God woke the flowers, getting our "cans reprimanded," as the drill captains liked to phrase it. These "reprimands" were often physical, usually without reason.

We were allowed to fight back, but really we couldn't. Once, on a three-mile grunge course we often footed across snowy mountain slopes, three recruits lashed out at Captain Sykes when he kicked over the thirty-kilo missile sphere they'd carried almost two miles. I empathized with their anger since I carried an identical sphere on my back while Reeves and my bunkmate, Ingrim, supported it with all their might to keep me from collapsing. If the missile sphere touched the ground, we had to start over. Plus, we couldn't quit unless we threw up or passed out.

Retaliation was an unfortunate misstep. The recruits suffered the most efficient ass thrashing I've ever witnessed. Bones were broken, and the next instant, I watched them writhing on the ground, screaming in pain. I made a metal note: "Do not engage in combat with drills captains. They enjoy this immensely for sport."

Before we were transported there, they confiscated everything we owned. High in the icy mountains, we had no contact with the outside world and were entirely at their mercy.

Grueling months passed, all to condition us for what came next. We were extracted in small teams and carted out to the Forests armed with nothing but sabers.

For Nahzir's sake.

In my squad there were eight of us, an air rig full. "Head west," the pilot yelled, standing beside the open door. "Report to Nahzir's Gate at Starlight City." I looked at Gaines to my right. He adjusted his parachute pack, trying to fit it over his lanky arms as beads of sweat rolled to his blond brow. He was nervous about the jump.

Nix, the oldest in the squad, flashed a metallic grin.

"See you ground side, Calhoun," he said, diving out the bay door. We parachuted through trees of the overgrown forest swamp.

That first night was pure horror, drifting through a dark world, threatening and unknown. Our orders were simple, but we didn't realize we were so far from Starlight City, and less than an hour into our hike through the tall swamp grass, we encountered something gruesome. I clutched my saber's grooved handle, almost losing my bowels at the sight of it – a faceless, humanoid figure that crept from a cluster of faintly glowing brush. The creature seemed to partially exist, it's extremities fading and reappearing at random, like those old-fashioned holos when the batteries run low.

My man Ingrim was closest; it went for him first. He was a durable kid who'd held his own at camp, but now he was a deer in the headlights, too spooked to move. The creature whipped its claws through his fatigue vest. He held his arms to his stomach, his dark eyes wide in shock as he dropped to his knees, staring at his blood.

"Ingrim!"

I'd yelled his name without realizing. The creature turned its black eye sockets on me, and Nix's saber plunged into its neck. Dust clouds puffed from the wound. The sight of vulnerability set something off in us. We attacked like hyenas, clawing and hacking, letting our fear turn us savage.

By the third day, we weren't shocked at the things we saw. Lee had pointed down the muddy path we were on, shielding his eyes from the blazing sun. We stopped.

"Look," he said. I squinted my eyes. Something large and rotund scuttled toward us across the mud — a hairy, swine-like animal with razor tusks. "It's Nix's mom," he said dryly, his expression behind the dark hair in front of his face unchanging.

We snickered.

It attacked us then. We lost Gaines in the fight and were down to six. By then, we'd killed maybe a dozen of these Forest creatures, none like the one that killed Ingram, which had dissolved into dust.

The last apparition we encountered was humanoid. We'd scaled down a coastal ridge where the river ended in a waterfall spilling down to a cove at the edge of the sea. Crystal-clear water gushed from cracks into the inlet where colorful birds perched on smooth stones sticking up from the water. Others pecked the pebbled white sand nearby. It was the most beautiful place I'd ever seen. I didn't even notice the creature standing at the mouth of a cave in the rocks until Gaines said, "What in God's...?" I looked to where he was staring. The creature was a human head and torso with tree limbs growing from it.

There was volition in its milky eyes.

"You rotting scum," it actually spoke dryly through blistered lips. Then, it came for us. I aimed for a fleshy spot at his neck, which wasn't flesh, it turned out. Even the human parts were tough like wood, and the jab left only a minor wound. But the hybrid man was slow, and we overmatched him by sheer numbers, our six-man squad quite efficient by this point. Only Nix and Wiliker dared to get within arm's length. While they distracted him, the rest of us struck at the tough wood of its flank.

My energy was thoroughly expended when Wilker paused, hands on his knees, sweat dripping off the ends of his long, tangled black locks and into the mud. The creature's black blood dripped from his saber. "Let's just leave it," he breathed. "It can hardly move now."

The hybrid man wouldn't die.

Hybrid men and mutant beasts weren't our only enemies. We battled hunger, afraid to eat any of the fruit blossoming on the trees – until around day seven when I could last no longer. I plucked a round yellow fruit from a tree overhanging large rocks near some rapids. The red juice inside was sweet and plenteous. The others did the same, and we consumed fruit after fruit from the tree. Bits of the furry yellow skin stuck to our palms and fingers. Juice dripped from our chins and spilled off our elbows.

After eating our fill, we camped by the river.

With the coming of night, I felt a growing discomfort. By midnight, I was sweating in droves. Then, I was shivering, as cold as ice. I touched a hand to my sore neck; it burned with fever. There was retching in my stomach, followed by unfathomable bouts of vomiting and diarrhea. The others experienced these symptoms soon after. Before long, I was sure we'd all die from the sickness. This lasted over a quarter rev, then my immune system began adapting. I felt my body stabilizing. In time, the sickness subsided. All but one of us made it. Mims was dead with vomit spotting his reddish beard.

"I'm sure it's the shots we had before training." Austin said, slipping his fatigue vest over his thick, pale white arms after he'd immersed it in the river, trying to scrub away the red stains. This was morn of the eighth day. I kept track of days compulsively. In a way, I think it helped me keep some of my sanity.

We'd all been silently contemplating how we survived the dire sickness. I remembered the shots – Hydra Resin injections, "Meticulously engineered," the white haired military doc at the med station had assured me after we'd been sworn in.

At Lee's request, Austin, Nix and I waded into the river, pulling Mims between us while Lee prayed over him. We released him into the swift current. Afterward, Lee sat cross-legged on the bank, staring over the water. Mims had been his bunkmate back at camp.

"May his body dissolve into the salt of the sea which gives life," Lee said, slightly louder than a whisper. "May his weightless soul rise into the waters of the Great Deep." He was silent then. Chirping insects and splashing water were the only sounds heard. I sat beside him, wondering what to say.

"I'm not too schooled in Nahzir's Doctrine," I blurted. "I was more of a Warfare Science guy."

"I'm sure it's a load of crap," said Lee. He stood, skipping a flat stone across the water. "Can't believe they sent us out here to die without telling us. The worst kind of betrayal." We listened to the water lapping at the rocks and fallen branches of trees leaning over the bank.

"I betrayed a friend once," I said. "Took something that meant the world to him. What kind could be worse than that?"

"You didn't send your friend off to die," he said.

Didn't think he might turn out to be wrong.

Traveling along the seacoast, we finally spotted the south end of the Diamond around dawn of day five. We pressed our way inland, across the plains east of the city, and approached the floating 'Link console in front of the Ether Shield. The rising sun reflected rainbow colors in the haze. I touched the console screen, noticing the oily grime caked under my fingernails and wedged into crevices and cuts on my hands. The other four recruits looked just as grimy. I could hardly tell, between Austin and Wiliker, who was the darker race and who the lighter, though I knew Wiliker was a darker brown than me.

"State your name and ID," a female voice in the console demanded. Nix gave his data. A squared portion of the hazy shield glowed like sunlight and vanished, leaving a clear path through the crystalline mist.

At Nahzir's Gate, Nix punched in at the lock panel. The huge steel door slid open just enough for us to fit through. We stepped across gridded metal toward a large, flat compound. At the right was a metal door to dispense military vehicles and hunter's rigs that scouted the Forests. Beside it, a glass door revealed an escalator inside.

The escalator conveyed us to another door.

"Place your ID tag before the scan ray," said a lively voice in the door speaker. Gaines was first, holding the barcode on his forearm to the scanner. The door opened. We followed suit.

A decontamination chamber was on the other side. Following the graphic instructions on the wall, we removed our blood-soaked uniforms and placed them in a chute labeled "Apparel," dropped our sabers into the "Weapons/Equipment" chute.

There were at least a hundred decontaminant cells. Naked and begrimed, I climbed into one, a steel sarcophagus with glass doors spread open. I switched the lever near my right hand like the directions on the arm indicated, and the glass folded over me. Restraints slide into place over my limbs, locking me in. Mechanical arms curled over the sides like tentacles with stingers. Long needles on the ends pricked into my arms and legs, my groin, my face and neck, through thin slots in the restraints. I held my breath as the cell filled with a warm liquid. Coldness rushed through me, intensifying in my veins until it was excruciating. My jaws clenched so tight I thought my teeth would shatter.

Then heat flowed through me, and an odd sensation, the feeling of release, like I was pissing uncontrollably.

The needles painlessly removed themselves, and the fluid flushed out through tubes under the cell. The light on the control module was blurry green coming into focus. It took some time to orient myself mechanically, to know whether I was backwards or upside down, and to maneuver my numb legs and arms.

With difficulty, I walked toward a door where Austin and Nix stood. Bright beams from the low ceiling scanned Austin from head to foot, flashing green sequentially. I fell in behind Nix to be scanned. Wiliker slid in groggily behind me, followed by Lee.

Glass cabinets lined the walls in the next room. Inside them were long robes of tanned hide, which we wrapped around ourselves to cover up. We exited through another clearance door and were outside at the Citizen Guard post inside the city.

NeoPilots in uniform were waiting for us, cheering as we approached. We entered the crowd of men and women standing along the walk. Some of them reached out to jostle our shoulders, or removed the hood on our robes to tussle our hair, swearing, shouting words of encouragement and praise. Some of us couldn't help smiling. We'd made it through.

Nix and I were assigned to Nebula Base in East One-Ninety-One. The others were stationed elsewhere. They restricted us to cadet training quarters for several weeks, but we'd earned back some freedom. We had these 'Link devices fitted over our forearms and could use them freely on our downtime.

When I synched mine to the Net and logged on to my NewStream account, tons of mail was backed up in my inbox –

hundreds of ads, and several feeds from soliciting corporations. One of them read, "Zahncorp Pharmaceutics is delighted to offer you a management position on our staff at the conclusion of your two-year service term." I suddenly realized what it meant to join the space fleet. A soldier was like a celebrity, someone who'd seen the Forests and lived to tell.

There was a feed from Randy too. After more than a week of fending for my life, the holiday incident had slipped my mind. I opened the feed:

Lu,

How are things? Thought I'd send a kite to see if you're alive. It's been months. Forgot how long you'd be gone. Hope you made it out alright. You're at Nebula Base, right? Melia got a job there last cycle doing data work. If you see her, tell her I said have a great life.

When you get back, we'll crack a bottle of the blue moonshine.

Randy

It bothered me that I might see Melia on base. Randy's ambiguous message bothered me even more. "Have a great life." I sent a return message saying things were looking up, and that I'd tell Melia if I saw her. Didn't hear from him after that. Of course I wondered if he knew about what happened, but there was no way to tell. It would eat at me.

One Saturn's Day, I was in one of the rec rooms on a meal break, and Melia sat down on the bench right across from me at the long table.

"Hi stranger," she said. There was a curious look in her brown eyes. For a few ticks, she didn't seem real. When I'd pictured this chance meeting before, I saw myself being angry, hurling accusations, demanding an explanation. But in the actual moment, no anger was there. Contrarily, there was something pleasant about her presence, a reminder of my former life maybe, before I was fully aware of life's fragility. Or maybe it was because I hadn't seen a woman out of uniform in months.

"Hey," I returned awkwardly. That holiday night flashed in my mind – the meeting of the masks. I remembered her breath in my ear.

"Randy told me you work here or something." I scratched the back of my neck, forgetting I'd been eating with my hands. Strings of noodle and bits of corn stuck to me. I brushed at it, and corn tumbled inside my collar. I left it there.

I'm a Decoder," she told me. "I weed out unreadable data on the StarMack interfaces and find programs to translate them." Silence followed. She looked out the window, then back at me. "So, congrats on making it through."

There was another flashback, this time to Ingrim getting sliced open by that ungodly creation. I blocked the image out.

"Why didn't you say anything?" I asked her. "That night, at the Gamma Club?" That's where we met during the Walking Dead festival. Again, she looked away.

"You knew it was me," she said.

"I swear I didn't," I replied truthfully. "But you had to know once we got back to my pad."

"What? I was sure... I thought when I said I lived by the base... you said you knew some people who lived in the district. I assumed you meant me."

"What about Randy?"

"We're not compatible. Everyone knows that, Lu."

She was right. We all knew. Hodge, Randy's cousin, had said it one night as we were leaving the Mulitverse Arcade a few years back.

"Opposites certainly attract," Hodge had said, repeating Randy's words. "But you and Melia are too far apart on the spectrum. You'll never reach a middle ground – not in this lifetime." It sounded cruel at the time, but maybe it was true. Randy was too reserved. Melia wanted more excitement from life than he could supply.

Cadets weren't to be seen with the opposite sex off base, and on free days, we weren't permitted to leave the district. But Melia lived in the district, so it was easy for us. On the three days a month I had free, we'd meet at the resident bar on the thirtieth floor of her building, then go back to her unit for some energy shots. Each time, thoughts of the holiday night invaded my mind, thoughts of physical contact between us. With each meeting, these thoughts became more vivid, and my imagination took hold, supplying fantasies. At these times, not once did I think of Randy. It was like my experience in the Forests had changed who I was.

Eventually, I acted on these thoughts, and Melia obliged. The first time lasted all of thirty ticks. I was surprised when she laughed, thoroughly amused. The subsequent times were better.

We saw each other for months this way, and I grew attached to the intimacy, needing it most when we were apart. I couldn't tell if it was love or lust. Maybe it was all the chemicals and hormones they injected me with. Whatever it was, I couldn't stop.

After cadet training, I was inserted as an Operant for the Interstellar Missile Deflection System, an entry-level pilot duty. Every day was a monotonous cycle of checking and quadruple checking launch parameters, making sure everything was in working order, that all strike ratios were in synch with stellar map coordinates. An uneventful job with no room for slacking off. The head Ops took their task gravely serious, but I knew no one could shoot missiles at Starlight City.

Then one day, Corporal Rigley, a head Op with six wings on his tan uniform collar, told me pilots of the "Conquest Fleet" had passed through the Sequiter and maneuvered into Earth's satellite field. The fleet opened fire on Harmonica's star base in an attempt to demonstrate the might of the Regime, to "bend them to our will," he'd added with a gleam of pride.

I just nodded, pretending to be as pleased as he was, even though I didn't know a thing about Earth or space combat and had no idea what the "Sequiter" was. Nahzir kept soldiers on a need-to-know basis.

Aside from that, it was a typically boring day.

That night, I was putting my rug sack together, getting ready to go off duty. I was supposed to meet Nix at Neon Bay Casino but got an urgent stream in my inbox from Melia. She sounded distressed, saying she needed to see me. I told Nix I'd have to take a rain check until our next off day. The message he sent back, nearly incoherent, conveyed something about him having the time of his life. Apparently, he was already fried.

I met Melia at the Café Shack by the port near South Main station. She was sitting at the sidewalk bar.

"Randy's gone," she told me. The orange light of the holo sign above the door showed concern on her freckled face.

"What do you mean?"

"He left a feed in my inbox saying he was leaving the city, going on about how he was through with everything."

"Leaving?" I asked. "Into the Forests?" The thought horrified me. Melia nodded. "He knows, then?" She nodded again, burying her face in her jewel-clad hands. Randy was as good as dead out there, I knew. No one could face that outer world alone, not without training.

I put my arm around Melia on the barstool beside me. In spite of it all, she loved him I guess. They loved each other. Wasn't that all that mattered? God, what was I thinking?

She pleaded with me to bring him back.

That following day, I sat with a team of Ops at consoles in the landing tower encircled by thick windows, drinking a Twinkle Soda I'd bought from the credit machine on the bottom floor. We were performing an atmospheric pressure check when alarms rang through the base. Our 'Link monitors switched on.

"Attention stationed units. Harmonica has deployed a return missile strike on Starlight City. All Ops, man a nearby console at once. This is not a simulation."

Before Corporal Rigley started snipping out his orders, I'd already clicked the flashing icon at the bottom of the image. Multiple missiles moved across the stellar map. But we had plenty of Ops. All I had to do was click an unassigned defense missile to activate it, lock onto a Harmonica missile that wasn't targeted, and engage when it crossed into the critical strike threshold flashing red on the map. This would be a slice of pie. I looked at Barnes sitting beside me.

"Let's splice some wigs," I told her. Randy's words had stuck with me since I'd left, and as I watched Harmonica missiles drift across the ocean of stars on the holo, my thoughts lingered on him. I asked myself the same question I'd asked Melia when I saw her in the rec room.

What about Randy?

I wondered what he said when Melia told him. After pondering all that time what to say if I saw him, now, I'd probably never see him again.

The beacon must have flashed for eight seconds before I finally noticed, thought, "Oh shit!" and clicked engage. Corporal Rigley screamed my name.

"Calhoun...Calhoun. You missed the fugging mark. You missed it..."

My heart skipped as I watched the screen. The Harmonica missile, an orange dot, moved toward Neon. The counter missile I'd fired, a flashing blue dot, skimmed by it with no detonation flash. My missile arched back and closed the distance as the orange dot penetrated Neon's satellite field, colliding at the very edge. Both dots flashed white and disappeared. By now, no other dots remained. I waited for a damage report, like an impending doom. The voice came through our 'Links again.

"All units. An interstellar missile explosion breached Neon's thanosphere. Starlight City may experience some falling debris. No civilian casualties are expected."

The Corporal stood over me. "Minor damage my ass. Nothing should have gotten through there. We can do this in our sleep, Calhoun. Have you got your prick in your hand over there?"

"No sir."

"Then what the hell happened?"

"Lost focus, sir."

"You're relieved of your position until further notice. Do you understand?"

"Yes sir."

"Report to the hangar, yesterday, or so help me God..."

And just like that, my tour was over. I never even got to sit inside a starship, let alone travel the cosmos.

I could have reenlisted after a full cycle. They'd have to put me through "corrective training," they said, whatever that was. I never found out. After being back home for only a month, I'd already found a niche: chimera hunting. I had to look for Randy in the Forests, even if I never found him. I started calling in to take any job that came up on the Hunter's Bulletin Net pages. If no one else signed up, I'd take on the jobs alone. "The Suicide Hunter," is what the news streams started calling me. But it was the only way my mind found peace.

I wasn't just searching for Randy, though. There was something about the outer world where horror and beauty exist intermittently – an allure greater than the everydayism of city life. I wished I could have been with Randy out there, experienced it with him. If I could find him out there, maybe in hiding, I'd teach him the way to survive. Then he'd see that none of it ever mattered, that it was all just petty details. Surely he'd understood that already, trapped in the Forests. I only hoped it wasn't too late.

For one job, I signed to a team of four hunters. Some scientist was paying megabytes for untainted breeds of any species. We rented an armored RV, an eight wheeler, painted shiny black with a turret on the back. After the fourth day of scouting, we hadn't trapped a single thing of value, nothing but mutants, stupid and hideous.

The same night, we came across three humanoids huddled together, overlooking a marshy creek bed. As we approached, they turned to us. There were no shrieks, no teeth flashed or claws drawn. They just stared, their faces warped and distorted like masks. The tallest of the three stared directly at me. Its elongated face and its drooping "O" of a mouth reminded me of the sorrow mask Randy had worn that night during the holiday festival. Like the first creature I ever saw out there, it faded in and out of reality. The thing reached its hand out to us, and Mike, the dark man beside me, promptly wasted it. The others creatures fled.

"You see that?" I asked, a bit spooked. "That was fuggin' weird."

"They're all weird, Lu," replied Mike. "Freaks."

"I'll wager that one tried to get through the Ether shield," Marcus said through his smiley-face mask. "See how it glowed? Creepy."

To this day, that face is stuck in my head. Always, it's fading, but it never completely goes away. A warped expression, an outstretched hand. I've had a different nightmare each night ever since. I just pray it doesn't haunt me forever.

E-Streams Extracted
Log-007..

Not sure who'd believe this. I can't find a data chip anywhere in the main components. It's been three weeks now that I've tinkered with this thing. I found the power circuit and ran it to the Omega power strip, then, removed circuits from one of the input slots on my StarMack interface, reordering them to correspond with the circuitry of the Stargazer© headpiece, which reminds me of Griffin's ThinkCap©. I put it on to test my wild hypothesis once I finally synched to the StarMack.

Right now, the holo image on my desktop is zipping through a virtual cosmos, and a caption in the background says 'Data stream detected.'

The StarMack is phishing through the CyberNet® for a program to decode the data. I've been waiting several phases at this point. Hard to believe it takes this long to locate one in all interstellar cyberspace.

Finally, a crystal cube appears. I maximize the cube. The logo of a corp. called Dreams Deterred lights up the top left corner. The colorful letters swirl like autumn leaves in the wind around the silver silhouette of a tree extending from planet Earth to the stars. There's no other info about the corp., just a queer passage beneath the logo:

Ideas supersede light's speed, traveling the void
back and forth through time. Unravel mysteries
of the mind –

Experience Simultaneity.

A flashing message says the data feed is being decoded. A second cube pops up in front of the one with the logo. My name is scripted across the cube – my barcode. Beneath that, various information about me – age, height, occupation – is listing off at random. The list continues; a third cube pops in front of it. Another message. It say's, 'Beneath that random information about me...' Wait, that's my... that's me thinking... 'Wait that's me thinking.' What? Christ, this is too much.......

Thomas Hurst -- NewStream Daily

Chapter 9

I didn't know I was asleep until rumbling in the tramway tunnel stirred me awake.

"Must be them," Lu said. He sat beside me on the ledge in front of the tram control box. Ike and Deacon had returned to the surface. Brushing cigar ashes from my lap, I stood as the tram rattled along the track, stopping in front of us. Hodge stepped from the lead car.

"Find any treasure, cousin?" asked Lu, grinning.

"You'd have to see to believe," Hodge said, walking past us down the tracks.

"Well, what's on the other side?" I had to know.

Griff stepped off and came toward us. "A flying city," he said.

In the days that followed, Ike and Hodge recruited residents to fight the Regime, mostly close friends and relatives. When other residents learned that Lu Calhoun was on Hodge's side, even strangers wanted to join. Residents gathered in the vendor's section near Deacon's unit, curious. They'd heard about people going inside the Diamond.

Deacon stood on wooden crates he'd placed together like a platform. From there, he preached to those gathered, and to those who passed curiously, telling them their troubles could end if they brought their families into the armory below.

"God's kingdom is at hand." He repeated on the second day.

"The enemy seeks to descend his wrath upon us. But salvation is not far. The spirit of God leads you."

People listened to him.

Once they actually started going into the armory, Hodge realized she'd need an faster way to get everyone inside.

"Make a bigger opening," was Griff's suggestion. We were trying to facilitate the flow of traffic, but the line to crawl inside had become a cluttered mess. I recognized the gray goatee with braids at the front of the crowd, the bartender from The Milky Way. He mumbled to himself about being bumped by people behind him.

"What's your plan then?" Hodge asked Griff. "We don't have explosives."

"I'll smash it," he pointed to the edge of the gap. "Move these people away."

Negotiating the crowd was tough. It wasn't that they didn't want to move, but there was no room for the ones in front to back up. Luckily, all the recruits had 'Link devices. Hodge gave me one that fit discreetly in my ear. We quickly got word to recruits to order those in the rear to back up.

Recruits and residents who'd gathered, a few hundred by then, watched Griff moon jump half as high as the cloudscrapers and crash down at the edge of the gap, splintering the concrete in a domino effect that stretched the gap at least fifteen feet across. He emerged with a leap from the avalanche cascading down the sloped barrack roof below.

Recruits helped clear the top balcony. We pushed broken concrete toward the edge where the tumbling debris had smashed through the railing onto a pile of ruble below. With the bigger chunks gone, I picked up loose shards and hurled them onto the pile. Two recruits had a contest to see who could throw a rock closest to the inner wall where the rows of lights shined like bright yellow eyes.

When word surfaced that the fugitive alpha human was with Hodge, everyone wanted to be a recruit. Soon, the upper balcony was crowded with people from the entire wall district. Miles held the sleeve of my coat as I helped Ike and Deacon support the heavy trunk they carried through the crowd. Naudica wasn't far ahead, leading Augie by a leash. We made our way to the gap.

Even with the gap widened, the only place we could step down was at the edge of the outer wall where the barrack roof was highest. Getting the trunk onto the roof without dropping it was a chore, but we maneuvered it down the broken rocks. Lu stood behind it, inching back to keep it from sliding. Reaching the roof's lower edge, we had another puzzle. We were too high to drop the trunk. Luckily, Griff stood at the broken section of the balcony rail.

"Hey, Griff." I called to him. He saw us struggling and lent a hand. We lowered the trunk over the edge to him and let go. He caught the falling end against his chest, leaned back to balance it and carefully set it down.

I worried the drop was too high for the kids, but they weren't afraid to jump. Miles's landing was rough. He scraped up his arm but said he was fine. I brushed pebbles from his small hands and his jacket. Griff stared at the trunk.

"Hodge needs more weapons?" he asked.

"My mom's in there," Miles said. Griff gave him a dazed look.

"I remember you," said Griff. "The Cathedral of Saints; I was with Jada," he trailed off, shaking his head. "Looking at your face just now, I saw one of her memories."

"Someone else's memory?" I asked, confused.

"I'm not sure." He seemed surprised. "Alphas can visit each other's dreams in Net domains set up for our C-conscious. With Jada, though, my connection's gotten stronger."

"Freaky," said Lu. Griff turned to me.

"Jada led the alphas that took your friend," he said.

"How..." I began, looking for an explanation.

"See for yourself." Griff slid the door open to the room where Hodge's lighthouse projector sat beside the crates. He ejected a silver jump drive from a slot hidden behind his ear, plugging it into the lighthouse. The projector eye shined virtual filing cabinets on the wall. He opened one. A video image appeared. A huge male soldier in steel armor with glowing gray eyes stood on a tram, his back to a window where city lights raced by.

"That's Bailey across from Jada," Griff said. "We're seeing through Jada's retina cam – her eyes, I mean."

The image swiveled to and fro, like someone was holding a camera.

♦

Inhuman Nature

Data streams across Jada's retinal display as she checks her task file. In these moments, the memories of Griff fade. Ever since he's gone missing, the memories have lingered, even shading over her consciousness at times.

Bailey stands before the seats across from her, his face statuesque, his gray eyes shifting their steel gaze. City lights shine through the glass floor beneath them. Through the window behind Bailey, maroon holos glow at Cloud Nine, a tavern on the air walk above Seola Street. A line of colorfully dressed city walkers is waiting to get inside. Their silhouettes blur with the tavern lights as the tram flies by.

"A decommissioned Regime soldier known only as 'Lead Eye' was spotted in West Four-Eighteen, a residential district," Jada silently reads on her display. This quasi-human is considered a threat to the Regime. Her team's orders are to detain him and bring him to The Zenith.

She blinks the display from her retina as the tram glides to a halt, glancing at Coral, whose waxy red hair flips in the wind blowing through the opening door between them. Coral nods as Bailey steps past them and waits on the platform near Macroware Plaza. Jada steps in front of him, her boots clanging against the metal surface. People sitting on benches near the cloudscraper's glass exterior, or leaning against the platform guardrail on the opposite side, take little notice of them, but a few in Jada's path scan her and steer clear.

Across the plaza, a narrow vector connects to a larger platform between three more cloudscrapers. A green sign flashes "West 418" at the end of the vector. They cross into the district limits, passing the Riff Raff Tav', where people sip drinks at patio tables with umbrellas.

Next door, a man steps from Hodge's Gadget Shop into the neon night, hidden by the shade of his hood.

At the end of the building is Supermarket 601, where a few city walkers push full shopping bins out through the wide doors. Jada reads the label on the corner of the housing unit beside the supermarket.

"Twenty-one E," she says aloud. "The next one's Twenty-two

E." She nods at the building to their left. "Our target's there."

Small children run up and down the stairs of the housing units with energetic laughter. A few older people sit at lounge tables along the wall, or on the ends of large flower gardens running the length of the building where magnolias grow amidst green foliage. Between two flower gardens, three men argue, crouched over playing cards spread before them beside a pile of shiny tokens.

Jada remembers playing this same game with Griff and the other alphas on base, when there were just four of them. They had no data coins to gamble with, only ten-gig jump drives. For a fraction of time, the memory is vivid, like she's in that very moment. It clouds her vision – the black metal walls of Griff and Bailey's quarters in the Alpha Bunker, and Griff sitting across from her, his green eyes aglow like Bailey's gray eyes, yet infused with something more profound, more alive than any eyes she's seen.

"The object of the game is survival," Bailey was saying. "But the ideal strategy isn't to save the highest cards. That's like hiding, which can backfire. The best approach to Face-up War is to systematically obliterate the enemy with calculated force. It's the same in live warfare."

"Can't say it's the same," countered Griff. "In actual life, every entity with power holds a card of diplomacy. Force isn't always the best tactic."

"He means in terms of actual combat situations," said Coral, leaning against the doorway. "Once you're engaged, the most effective strategy is a lot like Face-up War. I see his point."

"Live warfare doesn't work like a game," Griff returned. "Humans are involved, and humans have emotions. They remember things. Myriad consequences…"

This vision quickly recedes, the idea of it vaguely lingering in Jada's C-conscious.

Inevitably, she'll have to forget. She's made no mention of it to the neurotechs, but eventually they'll notice the abnormality in her C-conscious, and the memories will be deleted. Five cycles have passed since Griff vanished, twenty subtle shifts of the four seasons. He isn't coming back. She'll lose him forever. Perhaps she should get it over with.

The gambling men pause over lit pipes. Jada's slim physique is an illusion as she clanks along the platform. She shifts her eyes, analyzing the surroundings, scanning a street urchin approaching in a wrinkled, felt hat.

"Spare a few bytes?" he asks, removing the hat from his thick, matted gray hair and holding it open to them. They ignore him, continuing along the platform perimeter toward the third building.

A man stands in the doorway of Twenty-two E, hunched slightly, lighting a black clove. Jada approaches, and with the projector in her retina, displays a small holo she downloaded of Lead Eye, enlarging the image for the man to see.

"You, city walker," she says dryly. "Have you seen this quasi-human?" The man refuses to look up from his cloud of smoke.

"Who wants to know?" He asks.

"Withholding information is deemed inadvisable, city walker. If you know of this quasi-human's whereabouts, it is to your benefit to procure this data."

"I ain't fixing to tell you shit, lady, or whatever you think you are," he snips. Jada snaps open her forearm to release the Hexgun housed inside. The man jumps, dropping his smoke.

"I won't repeat the inquiry," she says in her flat tone. The man tries to hide his nervous twitching as he eyes the blue lights on the spinning Hexgun.

"You subhuman sack of – " His last word is cut off by a burst of shrapnel. He falls back, collapsing on the linoleum floor of the entranceway, blood pooling from his shattered skull.

They move through the doorway, stepping over the lifeless man. Inside, a boy wearing an oversized yellow poncho sits on the stairwell, frozen silent. Jada displays the holograph.

"Boy, have you seen this quasi-human?"

The frightened boy hides his face in his long sleeves. "I will not repeat the inquiry," Jada warns, lifting her Hexgun. She sees the boy nodding.

"He lives downstairs," the boy chokes out. "Fifty-one eighty-nine. Please don't kill me." Jada lowers her weapon.

"Your cooperation is appreciated. Stand aside, please." The boy runs up the stairs and down the hall, sobbing.

They head to the fifty-first floor two levels down. Unit 5189 is at the end of the hall beside a large window. A pink holo along the SkyTram railway in the distance outside reads, "Omega is clean energy, for a cleaner tomorrow. Jeaneen Ray, 2133." Spotting the West-17 tram racing along the railway toward the wall district, she's reminded of Griff yet again.

Jada turns to her team. "Forced entry is the logical course of action," she says.

"No room for diplomacy," says Bailey. "Can't let the target escape."

"So we agree. Weapons ready." She kicks the metal door off its hinges; it smacks the wall across the room. They flood through the doorway. A woman on the sofa screams, and a dark, wooly-haired man leaps from an armchair and darts into a back room.

"That's the target," Jada confirms.

"He's mine," says Bailey, stalking after the man. The woman on the sofa grabs a firearm from a nearby desk and aims it at him. Jada locks on the target, starts to fire, but stops upon seeing the woman's pale and terror-stricken face. She recognizes her.

The woman fires a concussive blast. The fiery shell barely misses Bailey, blasting a hole through the wall as he darts into the bedroom. To Jada's right, white sparks burst from Coral's mecha arm, a steel sickle. Sparks dance across the woman's body as she collapses to the floor, shivering, then, lay still. Jada feels electricity vibrate her face.

"What's your malfunction?" snaps Coral. "See that weapon she's holding?" She points to the woman lying on the floor, still clutching the weapon. "Regime-issue G-16 burner. The heat rounds in those can substantially damage our external frames."

"I've seen that woman before," says Jada.

"That doesn't alter you judgment. I'd dislike having to tell the Administrator you're an unfit leader."

"I've noted your concern."

Bailey returns, clutching a limp body in the metal claw on his right mecha arm. He tosses the man onto the mangy carpet – the man from the holograph; his human eye is closed. The blue lens in his left eye socket is diffuse, staring blankly. The skin around his cheekbone swells blackish purple.

"He tried to get out through the window," says Bailey. "I hit him with a tranquilizer blow, right to his flesh jaw. Knocked him out cold. Organic humans are more fragile than I imagined."

As Bailey examines his claw, fascinated by his own strength, a boy in a blue night suit appears from another room down the short hallway. In the leisure room, he pauses upon seeing his mother. His small hands begin to shake, and soon the rest of his body. He screams.

"Look what you did to her," he wails. "You killed her!" In the midst of sobs and screams, he pulls the weapon from his mother's hand. It's heavy for him, but he looks to know how to use it. He turns the barrel toward Jada.

"I'll kill you!" he screams, shrill and deafening. "I'll kill you for what you did!"

In Jada's C-conscious, another memory jogs...

At the Cathedral of Saints, Griff had picked up an old book about Harmonica, Earth's spaceport city. "Look at the symbol on this flag," he'd said, showing her the colored picture on the worn page. "I've seen it before." Back then, they hadn't downloaded data about human history on Earth, nor about earthling inhabitation of the planet Neon via The Sequiter, a wormhole discovered by Nahzir's father, which bridged two galaxies. She wondered when he'd have seen the strange flag – wondered many things about Griff, in fact, yet found his strangeness alluring in some unexplainable sense.

The boy had approached them, staring. Griff closed the book.

"Are you a lady cyborg?" the boy asked.

"Here we go," Griff muttered, walking away, between rows of tall bookshelves. City walkers tried his patience. It was their ignorance that bothered him, he'd said, because "their minds are programmed just like ours."

"You're very observant," Jada answered the boy. "That's precisely what I am."

"Shiny," he exclaimed. His mother appeared, grabbing his arm.

"I said it's not polite to talk to strangers. Get over here – I'm sorry, miss."

"No apology is needed," Jada assured her. The woman hesitated.

"Are you really a...cybernetic being?" she asked.

"That's correct."

"My ex-husband used to be a soldier. He says they're making heartless humanoid machines. You don't look like one of them. You seem rather friendly."

"Friendly?" Jada considered the word, trying to figure where it fit logically.

"I told him they can't all be bad. Let's go, Miles. It was good to meet you."

"Yes. Good to meet you," Jada repeated. The woman hurried off, pulling the boy behind her. He still looked back at them.

"Heartless machines," Griff said, standing next to her. "See what they think of us? They can't tell we're human inside, exact copies of their data, or that we're programmed to kill for them so they can be safe."

"Perhaps not," Jada replied. It wasn't the strangest thing Griff had ever said. Once, he told her he had a body of flesh and blood locked away somewhere, and that she probably did too – that all of the alphas did, all four of them – and that they had walked around in these bodies some years before. She had no memory of such an existence, only the cycles since her inception. Griff was the only alpha who ever spoke of such things, and such things he only spoke to her – and to Tom Hurst, the one who'd created their CyberNet brains.

The boy still looked back as his mother pulled him out the door. . .

The memory fades in a half tick, but the same boy's face still stares at Jada, tears streaming from his eyes. She scans the boy behind the burner. There's a foreign sensation in her neural circuitry she can't describe. The infallible logic she's always understood, that she can fold inside-out in her mind, fails to calculate a satisfactory course of action, but she knows the others are waiting to see what she will do.

Seeing only one option, Jada does something she's never done before. She closes her eyes, then, fires.

E-Streams Extracted
Log-008..

The mind is like the universe. Perhaps it is the universe. I see it now. With that head unit strapped on, my present-most thoughts appeared at the center of the text cube, and thoughts previous to that began spelling out down the cube. New thoughts listed themselves up the cube.

At some point, I couldn't tell if they were my own thoughts, or if something was putting them in my head. I could have scrolled up and down the cube with the nav orb, reading any thoughts I wanted, and rethinking them, I guess, but I was terrified and yanked the damned thing off my head. It's one thing to be able to play your thoughts back from the day; it's another thing entirely to read them as they're created from -- who knows what? Ether?

At any rate, I know how I can save Griffin. The anticode isn't the answer. Just need more time now.......

Thomas Hurst -- NewStream Daily

Chapter 10

"This plan is questionable," I told Griff. He was locking my arm to a metal restraint in Lu's armored RV. "I'm not seeing a way out of this for me."

"I've analyzed this scenario numerous times," Griff assured, clamping the other restraint in place. I still wasn't convinced, especially since the plan involved me turning myself over to Nahzir.

Back at the armory, while Griff and Hodge went over the plan they'd devised while they were gone, I'd been immersed in Jada's conscious stream and wasn't paying attention. I wasn't too thrilled to hear I'd been volunteered as the bait, needless to say.

Yet here I was, strapped to the wall cage in the cockpit of Lu's RV where he usually held captured specimens. Griff left through the cockpit door to the middle compartment, and Lu typed a code on his dash screen. In seconds, a fair-skinned woman appeared in a leather ball cap with a 'Link device on her ear.

"Calhoun?" she winked and saluted. "It's been a while. You go on vacation?"

"Something like that. Guess what I've got?"

She looked searchingly at Lu, then her eyes widened.

"You've got to be kidding," she said. "You found Nahzir's specimen?" Lu nodded cockily. No wonder the guy had his own show. He was some actor.

"You're the luckiest fool alive, you know that?" she said. "Hang on. I'm supposed to call my superior." The screen turned white with a "Standby" caption. Moments later, she reappeared.

"I've been told to patch you through a secured link. You'll deal with the Regime on this one." She saluted him with a grin, and her face was gone. Another woman appeared, mocha-toned, with a powder-blue lab coat. Diamond studs lined the arch of her left brow.

"Calhoun? I'm Dr. Jung. Administrator Nahzir will speak with you momentarily and instruct you from there. He'll want to see visible evidence of your claim."

The screen went blank. Griff was right. Nahzir would make the arrangements himself.

The screen flashed to Nahzir's ancient face behind a clear, plastic-looking mask. He had a long, grayed goatee, and slim, colorless eyes.

"I understand you have something of value to me." His filtered voice buzzed through a speaker on the chest plate of the thin carbide and polymer suit armor he wore. It was the same otherworldly voice I'd once heard in half-conscious dreams, floating in a glass prison.

"Yes sir," Lu replied.

"Let's have a look." Lu's net cam eerily turned on its swivel above the dash, apparently under Nahzir's control, searching, until it pointed at me and froze. A chill ran through me. Lu came over to remove my hood, and Nahzir stared at me in silence for some time before finally nodding.

"You don't know how grateful I am," he said, his eyes shifting back to Lu. "Though eighty gigs gives you some vague idea. Report to the gate console at sunrise. A convoy will escort you to an undisclosed location. Do not enter the city." The screen fluttered, and Nahzir was gone. Then, the entire dash console shut down.

"The hell did he do?" Lu wondered, holding up his hands, confused. He touched buttons below the row of screens to reboot them as Griff returned, unlatching the restraints to free me.

"They'll take you to The Zenith," Griff said.

"Zenith?" I asked. "That's where they took Lead Eye."

"You've been there before. It's north of the city, in the Argyle Mountains. You'll remember once you see it."

Starlight City

I put in the dark shades before Lu and I hopped out the rig's cargo hatch. We stood on the grounds at Hunter's Camp, a high, squared iron platform surrounded by a muddy trench in marshlands thirty revs east of Starlight City. The platform was encircled on all sides by an electric fence. At the north end, a ramp crossed the wide trench to the camp entrance gate.

RVs lined the west end of the grounds. Some, like Lu's, were painted in fatigue colors. One had red and green *Strike Zone* logos on the sides. Another advertised *Lenny's Pub* beneath a foaming beer mug. Probably half of the RVs were just plain steel, and some had multiple cargo doors.

Chimera hunters stood around a stone fire pit near the center of camp, enjoying themselves, drinking beer from silver cans. Slabs of meat smoked on a large grill hung over the flames.

A couple vendors had set up near the fire pit, selling customized apparel. One guy had worktables where he repaired gear and weapons with power tools.

We approached the cache machines lining the east fence, stocked with weapons and other necessities, like Hydra Resin Injections, which kept deadly sicknesses at bay.

"Shipments come in often," Lu said, standing before the locked weapons cache.

"You'll need a stronger tool than that Colt you're carrying. Wouldn't do much good against a hellhound. You'd need at least a fifty cal with shrapnel fire."

Behind the locked window of the cache, a Zeta .17 photon burner caught my eye, a shiny one, with the fifty cal attachment, like the one I'd carried years ago.

"How about that one?" I pointed.

"That works. Hey, it's limited edition. Only two thousand kils. I'll get it for you." Lu swiped his card through the machine slot. The burner turned on a dish-shaped mechanism and a clear panel opened. The metal locks around the weapon unsnapped. I held it in my hands.

"The photon pulse takes fifteen ticks to recharge after fifteen revs of use," Lu began.

"And thirty seconds to refill after a hyper beam," I finished. "This has the fifty cal attachment. That's why it's limited edition. I've used this burner."

"Yeah?" asked Lu, surprised. "Well good. Give yourself enough distance from your target, and a hyper beam will take down just about anything you'll see out here."

"Except an alpha human," I said. Lu paused.

"So they've claimed," he replied. "I can't picture anything absorbing that much energy without exploding. Besides, I'm assuming Griff has the alpha situation handled."

"He's only one guy," I said. "How many you think there are?"

"Four of us, originally," said Griff's voice behind me. We faced where he stood beside a huge cargo rig. His green eyes glowed beneath his hood. "Now there are six."

"And you plan to run through the other five?" I asked. His sharp-featured face actually formed a smile. That was certainly a first.

"That would be fun but impossible. They'd tear me to pieces, eventually."

"Reassuring," I replied. "The hell happens to me if they kill you?"

"I'm playing a joker card. You know Face-Up War?"

"Played a few times," said Lu. "I'm no good."

"It's not the greatest analogy," Griff said. "But it's a game of logic. Basically, the alphas won't question whether I'm a traitor if I go against all five. But with two in tandem, the logic ratios change."

A few hunters wearing space army suits eyed us as they went by. We paused, waiting for them to pass, hoping they hadn't overheard us. One nodded at Lu, who saluted him casually.

"Some will react emotionally," Griff continued once they passed, "which blurs logic. Confusion will lead to total malfunction."

"Why haven't more of them turned on Nahzir like you?" I asked.

"The alpha human mind is programmed by symbols, just like any robot or computer. Nahzir molded their minds the way he wanted."

I wasn't sure how to respond. It seemed illogical to me, and I expected things to go awry. But at least this was for Lead Eye.

"And you're sure the girl will join our side?" asked Lu. Griff was silent, as if reminded of something. He looked toward the stars in the clear but humid night.

"Jada visited my C-conscious today," Griff said. "She still has her memories." Lu leaned against the tire of the tall cargo rig, glancing at me with confusion. I probably wore the same expression.

"Even though the others were blank slates at inception," Griff went on, "their brains can store and retrieve data with perfect accuracy. Everything I've ever told Jada is a part of her thought process."

Pondering his last few words, I wondered if we could be part of some intricate thought pattern as I gazed through the fence beside the weapons cache. In the swamps beyond, silhouettes drifted amidst the trees; florescent eyes watched from the gray shadows.

E-Streams Extracted
Log-009..

    Michelle Jung's face popped up on the face chat while I was at my StarMack daydreaming again. Still haven't slept much. When I clicked on her stream, she looked flustered. Those pretty diamond studs on her left eyebrow were scrunched in a curve. She told me Regime officials had come to get Griffin's body. I told her to stall them anyway she could, placing a burden on her that was unfair, I'm afraid. In any other circumstance, I wouldn't have asked. She stood by me in the hailstorm the newscasts rained on me – the rest of them turned their backs. Even now, they pretend I'm crazy, when they supported me at first, those spineless – never mind them.

    When I got there, I found Michelle joking with the two swindlers in the lobby. They laughed at something she'd said. I ducked behind the two white sofas at the edge of the bright blue carpet, the ones facing the tall windows. Creeping past, I slipped down the near hall and through the entrance to the walkway. I could see treetops in the courtyard far below through the glass. A girl was seated at one of the small round tables along the wall. The late day sun glinted off a flower hair clip holding up her jet-black hair. Her face was intently focused on a notebook screen in front of her. She never looked up as I hurried by.

                                      Thomas Hurst -- NewStream Daily

Chapter 11

Griff went his own way once we left Hunter's Camp, and Lu headed west toward Starlight City.

"Get on the turret and check around," Lu said as we drove through the swamp. "Guys I know have been ambushed on this pass." I sat at the turret controls behind the driver's seat, swiveling the cam to get the feel of the analog stick, surveying the surroundings. I half expected to see something hideous like Lu had described in his story. Besides some exotic looking birds, though, I didn't see much.

Closer to the city, we crossed a shallow stream where I spotted a deer bent down to take a drink. She paused, looking over her shoulder at us.

"Holy freak of nature," said Lu, taking off his shades to see. "A pure breed? That's worth over twenty gigs. How does it survive out here?"

"Adaptability," I muttered.

Emerging from the Eastern Pass, we could see the ocean far to the south. We crossed the plain at the eastern side of the Diamond where colorful wildflowers grew. Three armored rigs waited in front of the floating console outside the Ether Shield. Each had roof turrets at the front and rear. A masked soldier stepped from the rear rig as the two in front slowly pulled away. He pointed for Lu to follow before getting back in.

Lu trailed them across the east plain, which stretched for miles along the shield. North of the city, we followed the convoy, circling a peninsula of trees to a hidden trail.

"No hunters I know ever go north," Lu said. "We stick close to the camp. Go too far from there or the city and you're in a dead zone. No signal out here."

We traveled through woods most of that day, crossing green meadows and calm streams now and again. I spotted remnants of paved roads overgrown with shrubs and odd-shaped, rusty tin houses with broken windows sitting near streams. Tall trees closed them in. Lu had no clue who had lived in them. "Maybe the ones who built the Diamond," he guessed. Putting the RV on autocruise, he pulled a deck of cards from a dash compartment.

"So you've never played Face-up War?" he asked, spinning in his chair to face me. He opened the deck and began to shuffle it. "It's an adaptation of an old game called 'War.'"

"War?" I said. "Everyone knows that game."

He dealt me ten glossy cards. "Lay a row of five cards face up," he said, "any five you want, and keep five in hand." I glanced at my cards. Playing a mixture of high and low cards seemed to make sense. I laid down the king of Hearts, then the two and ten of Clubs. Next I played the jack of Spades and the eight of Diamonds. Lu had already chosen his.

"So normally, the game starts when the last card is down, but I'll explain." He pointed to his row of five. "You can play from your hand on any of my cards if yours is higher, and you can choose to keep the book or give it to me. The idea is to keep the higher cards and give the lower ones to your opponent. If you're caught cheating, the other player wins."

"Oh yeah," he added. "When you lose a card, lay another one in its place. If I take all your cards, the match is over."

Lu won a few hands, then I won, then he won another. The first round was a race to get rid of our cards and win the highest books. The second round was a game of War the old-fashioned way using the books we'd won.

Meanwhile, nothing but endless forest drifted by in the arc-shaped windshield. Lu found some good music on the satellite, a compilation of Jay Dee tracks, centuries old. One was called "Love It Here."

"The songs of our ancestors," Lu had said with satisfaction. He played the station for hours until something scattered the signal. By then, it was past midday. Trees were sparser, and there were steep hills and valleys. The snow-capped Argyles rose and fell from view in the distance.

Long after sunset, we reached the Argyle foothills where a wide valley stretched on the right. Below, I could see rivers winding through miles of forest. Reluctantly, I let Lu strap my arms to the metal cage restraints again as the RV trekked up the mountain. Scaling higher, we started seeing more evergreens along the path.

As we finally neared the summit, snow-covered pines surrounded us. We rounded a cliff, spotting a gated bridge that crossed a steep cleft to a somewhat level piece of land across from it. A wide steel door there led into the mountain. I couldn't see past the rig in front of us once we started across the bridge.

The convoy stopped maybe halfway across, and masked soldiers stepped out. One stood on the driver's door ledge and tapped the side of the windshield. Lu slid the barred window open.

"Let up this side hatch," the soldier said through the mesh screen. "We'll get the cargo." Lu opened the cargo hatch with another button and came toward me as soldiers rushed in pointing burners at my face. He undid the restraints.

"Nice and easy," one soldier said as I cautiously stepped out. More stood outside. The steel door in the mountain had opened, and a pair of bright headlights beamed inside. Soldiers nudged me toward them. A hand touched the back of my neck, and a sharp sting ran through my arm before my body went numb. They carried me toward the tunnel as I faded out. The last thing I heard was, "Welcome home, freak."

Opening my eyes, I saw blue sky with purple streaks through a glass dome. Pink clouds drifted by, bathed in the setting sun. I felt I was slowly drifting too.

"You know why we gaze at the sky?"

It was his voice again, cold and hollow.

"Because life was born from a supernova."

The drifting stopped, and the pink clouds seemed motionless.

I turned toward the voice. A glare obscured the face across

from me. I sat up clumsily, my arms still numb. Nahzir and I were in the back of a driverless cart beneath a dome window. Through the windshield behind him, I saw white snow along a rocky cliff edge and rugged terrain far below. We entered another steel door, into a second mountain tunnel.

"That same energy exists inside us," he continued. "And it's still creating. Some call it the breath of God." I glanced through the window behind me. The convoy rigs were following us.

"The heavens call to our inner being. That's why they're so intriguing." He smiled. "Next subject. How's life after death?"

"What do you want from me?" I asked. The cart headlights revealed metal walls of the dark tunnel.

"Your body accepted the genetic compound my father composed for his Life Bomb. Just one regenerative HeLa cell from your blood can destroy any sickness. It may even bring humans back to life. We're one step away from immortality."

"Where are we going?" I asked.

"To the place you were recreated."

Through the mountain tunnel, a second gated bridge led to a high pass. White clouds drifted beneath us as we crossed it.

Anti-aircraft cannons peeked from the rocks at either side, angled toward the sky.

At a bend in the pass, a weathered face was carved into the mountain. It had a long, thin goatee, calm eyes, and looked almost exactly like Nahzir.

We entered the Zenith, a military base in the clouds. The terrain fell in rocky, uneven slopes to flat land below us. Railcar tracks curved through snow-splotched grass and rocks. On a far slope, immensely tall towers reached into the cloudless sky.

"That's where we're going." He pointed to the compound furthest right where two towers stretched upward behind a rounded glass facade.

Crossing flat terrain between, we passed soldiers' barracks and several wide, short buildings. In an empty field of snow, a platoon of soldiers wearing black muzzles and dark visors stood in drill lines, listening to commands from an officer wearing an shiny armored suit.

We climbed the opposite slope, heading for the Neuron Research Compound as an air cart whisked overhead. Nahzir's cart

Starlight City

crossed tracks at a railcar stop and slowed at a cement walkway leading to the glass facade. Soldiers from the convoy escorted us along the path as workers in civilian clothes curiously looked on.

Past the row of circular gardens extending down the center of the walkway, we stepped through the compound doors and across the padded rubber floor of the lobby. Display screens were everywhere. A winding escalator between potted plants and trees reached a glass upper floor where people worked at desks and StarMack interfaces.

We took one of the lobby elevators to floor sixty-three. Passing electronic doors with white nametags on them, we reached the end of the hall. I read the name on the last door to make sure it said "Thomas Hurst."

Around the corner, Nahzir decoded doors that read "Unit C." We entered a wide throughway with numbered labs facing each other. A guard stood at every door where workers in smocks moved in and out. At the end of the throughway, before a door to another hall, two guards stood before the Unit C Workroom.

The round door to the workroom spiraled open as we stepped toward it. One glance inside jogged vivid memories. This was the place I'd awakened from time to time behind a glass capsule, with Nahzir's voice prying into my subconscious, before I was set free. The back wall where the shattered cells had been was empty now, except for a chromium, humanoid skeleton beside a dry-erase board.

"I'm going to lock you in for now," Nahzir said. "We're anxious to get to work, but a pressing issue must be dealt with first, I'm afraid." I stepped inside. "Make yourself at home." The door closed behind him.

Now, I'd wait for a "signal" from Griff, whatever that meant. There was a StarMack interface in front of the curved railing. A gray smock was thrown over the chair. Making myself at home, I sat at the keypad and clicked the nav orb, searching through the data files and browsing the Net. I saw Hurst's "E-Streams Extracted" journal logs posted on the NewStream homepage; various documents in an "Omega blueprints" file cabinet; and some interesting text and video files in a folder titled "Rebirth," which Hurst may have compiled to document Griff's escape, and mine, five cycles earlier.

E-Streams Extracted
Log-010..

The walkway led me to the Cryogenics College. I'd visited the place periodically to see Griffin resting against the mechanical arm in the icing cell. He looked peaceful in his frozen state.

The thermo suits required to go in the preservatory weren't available at that hour, but I figured I'd last at least a few minutes without freezing. Had to take the chance. I slipped into the frigid room and hurried between the rows of icing cells along the wall. I usually didn't let my eyes wander to the other cells, but as I struggled to breathe in the freezing air, I found myself staring at some mutated monstrosity in a tube across the room.

One of its legs was remotely human, but the other was just a bulge of an appendage. The warped face was indescribable. I have trouble shaking it from memory.

When I flipped the lever on the module beneath Griffin's cell, it slid open. Cold air hissed out as the mechanical arm lifted him and carefully placed him face-up on a gurney that slid from the shelf in front of me. I zipped the plastic cover over him, then, struggled to slide the gurney off the shelf, as I couldn't feel my hands, or my face. The wheels extended, and I rushed for the door, pain in my fingers now, desperate for warmth.

It was nerve wracking trying to get out of the building. Anyone might have seen me and figured out what was happening. But everyone I passed by looked busy, or tired. Even Miss Zee, the building supervisor, just nodded her head when she passed me in the hall, yawning.

I was a nervous disaster by the time I made it back out to Saul's cart in the parking bay. The plan wasn't going the way I'd pictured – or maybe it was. I held out my digital recorder and played back Saul's voice from the conversation we'd had on his doorstep. He sure looked surprised to see me. Of course, I haven't talked to him since Anna died.

The voice activated lock on his 2158 Del Sol opened, and I slid the gurney into the load space after collapsing the back seats. The solar dial was still at half charge when I pulled off.

Thomas Hurst -- NewStream Daily

Chapter 12

Rebirth

◆

Hurst sat at the StarMack console in the Unit C Workroom, watching a rotating holo of an alpha human skeleton. The workroom lights had dimmed. He hadn't bothered to turn them back up. The room was lit by the holo, and by bluish light emanating from the fluorescent Hydra Resin fluid in the containment cells on the back wall, which held live specimens of the Rebirth project.

The hiss of the round electronic door surprised Hurst. He swiveled in his chair to see Nahzir step in.

"Jung told me I'd find you here," Nahzir said through his chest plate. His ochre-tan face was ancient behind his polymer mask, but his aged body was neurally fused to the machina shell that enclosed it.

"What are you doing?" he asked Hurst. "Uploads aren't until tomorrow."

"I'm designing a weapon for one of Griff's mech arms," said Hurst.

"Warfare Science handles that." Nahzir replied. Hurst switched the 3D image to a shiny, twin-bladed sword with a shotgun barrel extending between the blades.

"Griff found this toy on the beach when he was a kid," he said. "A little female action figure with silver hair. Her arm was a weapon just like this."

Nahzir watched the image rotate.

"His friends made fun of him for playing with a girl action figure, but he didn't care. It was his favorite toy."

"I've actually come to discuss Griff," said Nahzir. "Take a walk with me." Hurst followed him into the dim Unit C throughway, past several darkened labs.

"You know the magnitude of the work you've done since I brought you here." Nahzir began.

After a pause, Hurst replied, "It's not the first groundbreaking research I've done. There was Project Anna II, ten cycles ago. But you know all about that."

Nahzir smiled. "I've had eyes on you for twenty-some cycles now. You're a brilliant man, Tom. Your contributions help the greater good in ways you might not see."

"What happened to my prototype?" Hurst asked. It was Nahzir's turn to pause.

"An unsuccessful program," he said. "We sent her to Earth to capture living data for the Rebirth Project – fifty humanoids and various animal species. But the ship was nudged off course by something. We didn't know what. We had to call it back."

At the end of the hall, Nahzir touched the call button for the elevator.

"We found three dead Harmonica soldiers on board when the ship returned to Nebula Base. She killed four of our own pilots too. Luckily, a neurotech was able to fry her circuits with a CyberNet override code. She would have wreaked havoc on my father's city."

The white doors opened. They stepped on the bright elevator. Nahzir touched "seventy-six" on the panel and they swiftly ascended.

"A coding glitch," he went on. "But your CyberNet brain design allows us to duplicate A and C-conscious data. We don't even have to write programs now."

Hurst watched himself in the brass-tinted door.

"That's exactly why you brought me here," he said. "I don't see your point."

"You know anything about the soul, Tom?" There was an awkward pause. Hurst cleared his throat.

"Don't really think about that stuff, honestly," he said. "Not a spiritual man."

"Of course you are," Nahzir said. "Believing in science is like believing in God."

The elevator stopped abruptly at the roof level. They stepped into the freezing mountain air. Hurst dug his hands in his pockets and tucked his chin. His breath steamed thickly. He walked in stride with the taller man toward the edge of the roof where a walkway curved above a mountain rift, connecting to the tower of the Warfare Science compound. Snow clouds slowly eclipsed the starlit sky. Hurst sensed a storm blowing in.

"You believe mysteries unravel through discovery," Nahzir declared. He placed a withered hand on Hurst's shoulder, raising his other carbide arm toward the sky.

"They're infinite, Tom, these mysteries." he uttered. "The universe has no end. Science explains mere fractals of the highest reality, which no man can put into perspective."

Hurst shivered in the cold silence as Nahzir gazed at stars not yet covered by the approaching front.

"What's this got to do with Griff?" Hurst asked.

"The consciousness isn't data you can just copy. It's energy. Souls are energy, Tom, with a capacity for creation and destruction. With control of such energy, we can accomplish things unfathomable."

"Not sure what 'things' you're referring to," said Hurst. His teeth were chattering. "It's dreadful out here. Can't we go inside?"

Nahzir touched the scanner on the steel door and stepped in the heated walkway. The lights were dim. They could still see stars through the arched glass.

"I used to wonder what purpose these capacities served – creation and destruction – and could never come to a satisfactory answer. But the answer is so simple."

Hurst rubbed his numb hands together. Nahzir wasn't disturbed by the cold.

"Let's hear it then," Hurst said, blowing into his hands.

"Perfection. Energy seeks perfection. Hence, an endless loop of construction and destruction."

"There's an abstract concept," Hurst chattered. "You can't give evidence for such ideas."

"Energy makes quite an investment in the humanoid races, don't you think? Because we're destined to be a perfect race." He stared at moonlit mountaintops in a sea of darkness.

"But a perfect race is self sustaining," he continued. "And when the selves interfere with sustaining, the race becomes self-destructive. Only the whole of something achieves perfection. The parts themselves are imperfect."

Hurst sighed impatiently. He wasn't interested in Nahzir's Doctrine at the moment. He wanted to know what this was about. Nahzir faced him.

"Since their inception, Griff has exhibited a very individualized sense of purpose. I've seen him in combat sims. He feels he's mentally superior to them. That's why his team is usually the victor. Physically, the alpha male-female pairs are interchangeable.

"Maybe he remembers what it's like to die," Hurst argued. "So he fights to live."

"There's the trouble. His memory." Again he faced the glass. "I'm afraid it has to be wiped. He shows a flawed way of thinking, which I simply can't have."

"The hell do you mean?" Hurst glared angrily. "You told me I could bring him back to life if I helped you build your fugging super soldiers."

"But you have brought him back," returned Nahzir.

"Without memories, he won't be Griff. He'll be...a blank person. The bond I have with my son will be broken."

"You'll form a new bond."

"You've had this whole ship rigged from the start," Hurst said, tears of anger burning now. "You said..." he trailed off.

"I truly am sorry, Tom. But I must do what's necessary."

"You're a Darwin freak," he said, turning away, fists clenched. "You think you're Nietzsche's Overman, god of this pitiful planet you're father ruined. You think I haven't figured it out?"

"Tom, you misunderstand. I'm not out to dehumanize man or any such nonsense. All can live harmoniously. Happiness is a mere state of mind."

Lying in bed late that night, Hurst stared in the ceiling mirrors and asked the silence, "What was it for?" Griff would be just like the others, human in theory – another copy of unintelligent conscious data inside a machine, ready to be programmed in Nahzir's Doctrine.

An alarm screeched outside Hurst's door. He sat up, startled.

"Emergency. All armed personnel to Workroom Unit C immediately. Repeat..."

"The hell's going on," he wondered. He'd just left Unit C not two revs before. He slipped his gray smock over his silk pajamas and touched the fingerprint scanner on his door. Yellow lights flashed down the hallway. He turned the corner beyond his room, touching another scanner on doors to the Unit C throughway.

As he passed a second sliding door, a fleshy, slug-like creature slithered toward him – a Rebirth specimen, no longer resembling the man it had once been. It flopped its heavy body onto Hurst, trapping him against the door, which had locked behind him.

Its contorted, rubbery face spewed saliva on Hurst, snapping long, razor-like teeth. Its jointed limbs tore at Hurst's smock. With his burly arms, Hurst held his attacker's teeth inches from his face.

Burners percussed loudly down the hall. The heavy body convulsed in Hurst's grip and collapsed. Hurst stumbled back, afraid to turn his eyes from it.

"Jesus," he shrieked.

"Nope. Just building security," said the soldier through his muzzle. "You alright, Prof?" He looked Hurst over, touched him on the shoulder. "You don't look hurt."

"I'm fine." Hurst wiped his face with the sleeve of his smock; then, he shrieked. The specimen had slipped behind the soldier. It lunged upon him. His visor snapped off the headgear of his combat suit and smacked the white tiled wall. Trapped under its weight, the soldier yanked a long knife from a strap at his leg and plunged it in a fleshy side. A webbed appendage cupped the soldiers face, and a claw forced its way into his eye socket. The soldier fluttered helplessly, a scream caught in his throat. Hurst fell back, shrieking, swearing. The back of his head hit the wall.

There was a barrage of gunfire. Hurst's ears rang from shock as shrapnel from both ends of the throughway ripped through the creature, jolting it like electricity. The firing ceased.

It was certainly dead now.

The hallway spun around Hurst. He staggered, held himself up on the wall and regained composure as soldiers rushed to their comrade. Hurst headed down the throughway, where more soldiers gathered outside the workroom. Still more soldiers chased something moving fast down the hallway beyond Unit C.

Hurst passed under flashing lights above the workroom doorway. Inside was an absolute wreck. The containment cells were shattered. Fiberglass shards floated in the fluorescent Hydra Resin fluid on floor. The specimens were gone, every last one.

He rejoined the soldiers outside the door as Nahzir approached, pausing to stare at the disaster. Rage flickered in his eyes but quickly passed.

"Seems we have a situation," he said. "Someone care to explain what happened?"

"That alpha with the blade arms," said the soldier in front of him. "I saw him jump out the window when the alarm went off."

"Griff?" Hurst uttered in disbelief. Nahzir turned, seeing Hurst for the first time.

"And the devil appears," Nahzir said quietly. He turned without another word, making his way back up the throughway.

The next day, everyone in the compound had seen the footage on one of the lobby screens. Hurst stood in the lounge on the tenth floor, watching it again and again on a screen in the table before him, watching Griff ransack the workroom in a manic rage, shredding the fiberglass cells, setting all the specimens free.

Now, he was nowhere to be found. He'd headed God knows which way over the Argyle Mountains.

A message streamed across the table screen. Several modified humanoids had escaped from The Zenith, it said. Nahzir would pay gigabytes to anyone who could detain them. Over the next week, the specimen's were singly tracked down. Regime soldiers captured or killed most of them in the mountains, and chimera hunters trapped a few just outside Starlight City. After Regime scientists confirmed the bodies, all but one of the Rebirth specimens were accounted for. The only successful result of the project had disappeared. Nahzir spiked the currency reward for this one to forty gigs.

He posted an eighty-gig reward for Griff – but soldiers knew what the alphas could do, and news traveled fast to hunters. No one had signed up for the job.

Hurst walked into his furnished quarters carrying his lunch in a perforated plastic dish. The door slid shut.

"I've sent the alphas after him."

Hurst jumped at the voice. Nahzir sat in one of three barstools at the front of Hurst's quarters.

"Only one way that ends," said Hurst, placing the steaming fish on the bar top. "He can't combat them all." He grabbed the nameless bottle of bourbon on the bar and poured himself a shot. Nahzir sighed.

"I made a mistake letting you oversee his recreation," said Nahzir. "I'm correcting that mistake." He stood, walking toward Hurst. "The only other option is to shut him down the way we did Anna II, but that would fry his neural circuitry."

Hurst averted his eyes. He'd had his friend Dr. Jung secretly disable the CyberNet override function from Griff's brain after the neurotechs encoded it.

Nahzir paused at the door, still looking at Hurst. "It's odd that they haven't tracked him yet, with their capabilities. If he's influenced them in some way, that will also need to be corrected."

Hurst looked at the floor. He'd never expected Griff to do something so extreme. Setting the Rebirth specimens free. People had died because of his actions. It wasn't like the Griff he knew.

"It's not your fault, I guess," said Nahzir, facing the door. "I've only myself to blame." He punched an access code on the panel beneath the print scanner, leaving Hurst alone.

Unable to find sleep that night, Hurst got out of bed, slipped on his fleece jacket and took the elevator to the roof. There, he stood alone in the cold, wondering where Griff would think to go. He knew why he'd gone – conflict of interest. Griff's cognitive patterns didn't line up with Regime ideology. He didn't believe in manipulation for the sake of some "greater good," as he'd expressed privately to Hurst.

Even as a boy, he'd always had a mind of his own.

Hurst had tried to reason with him, tried to persuade him to accept his new life, or to cope at the very least. It was the only way Nahzir would let him exist.

Thick clouds obscured the landscape below, enshrouding mountain peaks far in the distance. The world beyond was expansive and uncharted – untamed.

Where would Griff go?

If the alphas found him, they were more than capable of destroying him. Maybe it was for a better end. If he'd stayed, Nahzir would have erased who he was, supplanting a new identity. He'd be a blank slate.

A light snow began to fall. Hurst looked to the sky and began praying that Griff would go far away. Maybe he'd never see his son again, but as long as Griff existed, their bond couldn't be broken.

Starlight City

E-Streams Extracted
Log-011..

When I got back to the height's parking bay down on the street, Saul stood there in his house robe and slippers, looking more surprised than before, and angry. I tried to explain that I had a reason for taking his cart, that it was for Griffin and I didn't own one, which he knew, but who'd listen at that point? He turned white when I pulled out the gurney with Griffin hidden beneath.

Doesn't matter, though. I made it back. Griffin's here now. All I have to do is put the Stargazer© headpiece on his head. Wait – this can't possibly work. Can it? What if it won't work on someone in a cryogenic state? Man, just do it and stop hesitating.

I can hear someone knocking at the door. I'm not here right now, whoever it . . . My door's being decoded. Citizen Guards. Saul must have called them. But I'm not finished yet. Doesn't matter. They've opened the door. Can't hesitate. There's no more time. I need to get this on Griffin's head. They're coming down the stairs.

You can't barge in here. I'm not through yet. They aren't listening, and I've got no way out. They've backed me into a corner.

Look. I point to the StarMack's holo image. *The decoder is synchronizing with Griffin's conscious streams somewhere in cyberspace. I can bring my son back.* The guard closest to me doesn't even look to where I'm pointing. Instead, he turns to his partner.

Singh, they were right, he says. *Guy's a wacko.*

The nerve of this idiot, mocking me. He gets what he's paid for. My grafted fist slams against his visor. I whip him around, slam him against the wall. Caught the guard off guard. He squirms to get loose.

Shoot this husky son of a bitch, Singh, he yells through his helmet muzzle. The other one, Singh, laughs. He says something I don't quite catch.......

Thomas Hurst -- NewStream Daily

Chapter 13

Those clips of Hurst brought memories of my team flooding back to me. We'd all grown up as friends and became Soldiers of Peace together. I felt a hollow space on the inside. Tears burned as I thought about what Nahzir had done. He stole Hurst's prototype and ultimately had it kill us. At that moment, things came into perspective pretty clearly. I was their leader, and I couldn't protect them. Yet, they had only found three bodies, and I'd heard shrapnel in the corridors; someone had run for his life. What if he'd escaped? At that moment, I felt I had to get back Earth, had to find a way to see what I'd left behind.

After two revs, Nahzir still hadn't returned to the workroom. I stood from the StarMack, dazed by the memories. I walked the left curving stairs to the level below. The chromium skeleton stood against the wall – an "Alpha Model Frame," I read on the label above. The human-shaped head had a face with sharp male features. I rubbed a hand across the ribs, which had a coarse, adamant feel. The arms and legs were built from finely shaped rods and discs threaded together. They appeared fully flexible, with multiple bolts connecting each joint. The left arm was an intricate contraption of parts within parts. I touched a pressure latch on the elbow and jumped as the chromium arm snapped apart, taking the shape of a shotgun.

On a dry-erase board beside the skeleton was a hand-drawn diagram of a wheel with twelve notches, and arrows showing how they spun around a center point, like an Omega generator. At the top, someone had scribbled, "Alpha Human Heart."

Three machines that looked like arcade games sat beneath dark screens in the far wall. Otherwise, the workroom was empty.

I walked up the opposite stairs, checking the door again. The guards were still there. Again, I sat at the StarMack, sighing, shuffling through more of the endless files before coming across one called "City of Invention," with digital blueprints of city streets, motor carts, and 3D diagrams of cloudscrapers I could tilt at any angle using the nav orb.

An alarm screeched, and yellow lights flashed outside the workroom door. A voice in the ceiling said, "Warning. Alpha human X5-04 has been spotted on base. Soldiers on active duty, report to your commanding officers. Unarmed personnel, report to your quarters for lockdown."

That was a clear enough sign. I checked the door again. The guards had taken off. Slipping the gray smock from the chair on for good measure, I rushed to the door and keyed the code Griff had given me, "a-l-p-h-a-o-m-e-g-a." The orange light turned green, and the round door spread open. Men and women in similar smocks headed for doors at both ends of the Unit-C throughway. Many wore clean smocks, but some were stained red, oily black, or bright blue. I merged with the flow, heading back the way I'd come with Nahzir.

At Hurst's room around the corner, I punched the second code I'd memorized, "6-8-4-3," slipping in as the door opened.

Hurst was leaned back in a plush chair at the far corner with a ThinkCap like Hodge's clamped around his head. Magnetic wires connected it to a 'Link monitor sitting on his bed. Hurst's mouth hung open. His head was tilted back. I rushed to lift him by the arm and caught his head as it sagged forward. His eyes were blank and lifeless. I pressed two fingers beside his Adam's apple and found no pulse. On the 'Link screen was saw a caption reading, *Upload finalized*.

I had to go without him if I wanted to get out of there. The elevator took me to the ground floor. I froze as a crowd of people rushed onto the padded floor of the lobby. They were all rushing to the elevators with worried faces. Dodging through the surge, I walked out the door discreetly, past the row of gardens toward the railway stop. It was dark out now, except for the soft lights outlining the gardens, and the lights inside the glass facade of the compound.

Soldiers escorted a few people in smocks toward the entrance. One was a familiar face, the mocha-brown woman with diamonds along her brow who'd spoken to Lu on the RV screen – Dr. Jung. We made eye contact, but she kept moving.

Passengers emptied the railway car on the tracks. After letting them pass, I stepped on alone. Interior lights along the windows darkened as the car pushed off. Sitting in one of the seats, I considered calling Griff on the 'Link before remembering he'd specifically said, "Don't turn it on until you're near the bunker."

The car sped past another compound with tall towers and up the slope of the valley, racing over a stretch of flat land at the top and down the other side. Griff said the Alpha Bunker would be the next stop, so I assumed the metal platforms extending from the mountain slope below were part of the bunker, which went deep into the mountain.

The railcar looped around the platforms and stopped between orange and green light posts below. When the doors opened, I ran through the snow to hide among the evergreens nearby, climbing back up the mountain slope. From a good distance, I stood level with a steel door that led into the bunker. A group of soldiers stood on the platform in front of it.

I touched the 'Link device inside my earlobe to turn it on. The call signal beeped immediately. I pressed it again with the same finger and heard Lu's voice.

"Black? I'm picking up a heat dot near the RV. I hope that's you."

"I'm in the woods," I told him.

"Stay there. I'll come get you."

The RV pulled close to snow-covered trees behind me. I stepped around them onto a flattened trail and climbed into the open cargo hatch.

"Griff said to wait here," said Lu, shutting the hatch from the dash console. "Hurst?"

I just shook my head, not knowing how to explain.

"Something's going on over there," he said, looking through the window toward the platform. "Some soldiers in front of that door."

"I'll zoom in on the cam," I said, sitting at the analog controls in the booth. I panned toward the soldiers and touched the "plus" icon on the screen to zoom.

"They're standing in a circle," I said.

"How many?"

"Five?" I counted. "No, six. Two inside the circle, counting that guy in the armored droid. Wait, that's Nahzir."

"The rest must be alpha humans," said Lu. "Flip the audio on. The mic focuses where you aim." I touched the speaker icon, and voices spoke through the dash monitors.

"The others have been evaluated," said Nahzir from behind his bipedal droid's glass shield. A chain gun was harnessed on the arm. "They believe your actions put them at risk on your last tour."

"At minor risk, Administrator Nahzir," Replied the dark-haired woman before him. I recognized her hollow voice. It was Jada from the clip Griff had shown us. She had intense violet eyes and olive skin. "There were three citizens," she added.

"Risk is risk," returned Nahzir. "But that's not the matter at hand. Malfunctions are easily corrected. You failed to mention your lapses in consciousness to the neurotechs. You hiding something?"

Jada was silent.

"Bring the target out," Nahzir barked, looking to his right.

"Sir."

I shifted to the voice – Coral, the one with blood-red hair and ivory skin. She moved toward the bunker door. It slid open as she approached.

"We'll dig to the bottom of this," said Nahzir.

Coral returned dragging a disheveled, shirtless man with a robot arm by his long black hair, shoving him to his knees before Nahzir. The quasi-man's tired face looked up.

"It's Lead Eye," I uttered with shock, looking at Lu, then at the screen again.

"We've no use for this quasi-human," said Nahzir, pointing his chain gun at Lead Eye's lowered head. "Dispose of him. It's what the GenPub wants. Prove your identity isn't compromised." Lifting Lead Eye with the droid's metal arm, Nahzir shoved him toward

Jada. Lead Eye fell to his knees again, glaring up at her.

"Do what's necessary," demanded Nahzir.

"Sir," Jada said. My heart jumped when her right arm snapped apart, extending a gun with six barrels of varying shapes. Her violet eyes met Lead Eye's stare for a pause, then looked to the ground. The whirling Hexgun retracted into her arm with loud clicks. The hand and forearm snapped back in place.

"Negative, sir," she said.

"You realize your identity will be absolved?"

"Sir."

Nahzir turned to the others. "Take her inside," he ordered. Coral and a male alpha with ultra-white hair escorted Jada through the electric door to the bunker. Two remained, watching Jada until the doors shut her in.

We saw a bright flash like lightening, heard a deafening bang and felt the RV rock from side to side.

"The...?" I started, looking up from the cam.

"Look," Lu pointed through the windshield to an exploding fuel tanker beside the platform. Rainbow flames set the night ablaze. Lead Eye hit the snow as black clouds billowed from a tanker that sat beside four others. Two more tankers exploded; gunfire rattled; sparks flared in the smoke. I got back on the cam. Griff stood among the flames, arms spread. His shock-blade arms flipped open like metallic wings.

Shrapnel sparked off his blade arms as the two alphas swarmed him. One was a dark, blue-haired girl firing Gatling guns from her elbows. The other was gray-eyed Bailey. His right arm had a huge metal claw and a rocket launcher attachment. His left forearm fired pulse rounds, forcing Griff back until he was cornered against a high wall at the edge of the platform. Bullets sliced Griff's skin as he rushed through an opening, barely dodging Bailey's claw.

Griff's attackers were on him at once, not leaving an inch to breathe, if he required it. He was on the bitter end, but there seemed insurmountable power in him.

The dark girl charged Griff head on. Bailey crouched to a knee, straightened his claw arm and fired the rocket launcher, hitting the mark dead on. Griff bounced off a steel wall in the mountain, skidding across snow on the platform. He was on his feet again as they cornered him, sporting fresh burns and scars on his face.

Grenades flew from the bunker doors. The alphas scattered. I swiveled the cam to see Jada rush to the platform. Coral and the white-haired alpha dashed from the doors behind her.

I found Lead Eye with the turret cam. He'd taken cover behind a row of metal drums not far from the door. I shifted back to the battle. White Hair turned his guns on the other three, siding with the minority. The others switched sides back and forth until the battle had split, three against three. Ultra-white Hair and the dark girl went berserk, attacking everyone that moved – total malfunction, just like Griff predicted.

"There's our ticket," Lu said, sliding forward in the seat and skidding off the trail. The RV climbed up the snowy slope around the platform. Speeding past the burning tankers, Lu stopped level with the platform, close to the battle, hopping on the turret as I leapt out the cargo hatch. Griff and Jada made zigzags toward the RV. Bailey cut off their path.

I circled the fight and sprinted toward Lead Eye lying in the snow beside a drum, covering his head. I pulled him up by the arm, and he wrestled away.

"It's me," I yelled. "It's Black."

"You?" He stopped. Bullets ricocheted off the drum, shooting sparks in our faces. We ducked down. "The hell's all this?" he asked.

"Nothing good," I said, looking for an escape. "Let's bail." I tugged him behind me, rushing past the barrack door toward the RV. Lu's turret swiveled to and fro, popping heavy shrapnel.

Nahzir intercepted our path, stopping us dead. His cold eyes stared at me in disbelief. "I never expected…" he said through his speaker. Lu's turret aimed toward him. We shielded ourselves as it sputtered shrapnel, shredded the right leg of Nahzir's droid. It collapsed as we sprinted by, hopping from the platform and around the RV to the cargo hatch.

"You working with alpha humans?" Lead Eye yelled above the noise.

"Sort of," I said, climbing in. Lu hopped from the turret and took the driver's seat.

"I ain't riding with those things," Lead Eye hesitated. I turned to him.

"Get your ass in. We got no time." I tugged his arm; he climbed in half-willingly. Through the windshield, I watched Griff and Jada leap onto the RV roof with heavy thumps.

"Take the gun," yelled Lu.

Lead Eye gripped the wall as the RV backed out and spun. I swiveled the turret as Lu peeled out across the flattened snow. The mountain shook as the other alphas fought in the distance. A red blur flashed at the bottom of my screen. Aiming down, I spotted Coral sprinting after us, sidestepping explosions of snow and rock set off by Jada's grenades.

She was closing in.

I fired and missed as she lunged at us. White light burst from the spinning sickle that was now her left arm. She smashed it against the RV. My teeth chattered, and intense pressure plugged my ears. A thunderous crack sounded above. The screens in the RV went haywire with static, then blanked out before flickering on again. Looking at the hazy cam screen, I watched the smoking turret barrel slide off the roof and hit snow.

"Holy freak," Lu exclaimed with shock. He kept his thumb on the accelerator. As Coral hurdled the severed turret, a grenade blasted her legs beneath her. She crashed sideways into the snow and disappeared as the RV hit a dip in the path. Lu veered right into frosty pines of the mountainside.

Jada and Griff climbed through the open cargo hatch, and Lu closed it. He shut off the headlights, driving through gray darkness.

"She can see in the dark," said Griff.

"She's on my scan," said Jada. "Shift course seventy degrees west or she'll intercept us." Lu looked at his screen, steering the RV around trees, decelerating down a steep slope.

"My dad?" Griff looked at me. I shook my head.

"His brain was swiped or something," I said. My head wouldn't stop shaking. The whole scene had just confused me. "I found him in his room."

Griff responded with silence at first. Finally, he said, "So he freed himself. Shouldn't have doubted his resolve."

E-Streams Extracted
Log-012..

    I was being dragged into a holding cell when I woke up. Pain throbbed at the base of my neck, and for a moment, I couldn't move. I was trying to figure out where I was when these bars slid shut. It all rushed back to me then. The Stargazer©, the guards, Griffin. They got what they were after.

    They haven't figured out what to do with me. Michelle told me as much when she came to visit me a couple days ago. She says the news streams are calling me a dangerous man. Imagine that. The GenPub is calling for the harshest sentence. Michelle says she doesn't know what that is. It looked like maybe she had an idea but was afraid to say.

    I'm allowed a GenPub hearing to make my case, but what's the use? The Regime wanted to silence me. They never wanted me to find the anticode, or to save Griffin. Some good it'll do to address the public. They'll just twist my words so I'll look more psychotic.

    I gave Michelle the code to my front door. She said she'd see what she could find. They won't allow me another visit until Friday, so I'll have to wait until then to see what they took from me.......

                                  Thomas Hurst -- NewStream Daily

Chapter 14

With Jada navigating, we reached the Argyle foothills without another encounter. Hours later, approaching from the northwest, we spotted the Ether Shield, a rainbow silhouette above the Starlight City skyline, glowing in the dawn.

"We can't get through the shield, Griff," I said.

"You can get through okay," he replied. "Lu can't. Neither can a quasi-human." He looked at Lead Eye.

"Don't worry. Calhoun has clearance," said Lu. "We'll have to drive around to the east, though."

"You're gate clearance is probably suspended," said Jada. "They won't let anyone in or out until they've tracked us. We'd have to shut the shield off to get you inside."

"Can we do that?" Griff asked her.

"The power grid's underground beneath the gate complex," she answered, "But..."

"That would leave the city exposed," said Lead Eye.

"There's the problem," she said. "I'll do whatever this quasi-human decides." She looked him in the eye. "I feel I owe you. Your ex-wife was killed under my command."

"By your hand?" asked Lead Eye.

"Once I recognized her, firing my weapon didn't seem . . . logical."

Starlight City

"My son," said Lead Eye, covering his face.

"Miles? He's fine," I said.

"What?" he looked up.

"I couldn't decide the proper action," said Jada. "That's why I was being evaluated by Nahzir. I didn't exact a fatal wound."

"Where is he?"

"With Hodge," I said. "I meant to tell you, but bullets were flying at us. I found him at your ex's place."

Griff opened the cargo hatch. "What's the verdict?" he asked. "Regime's on our tail. We shutting down the shield or not? Wall residents have either gone inside the Diamond or they've already been transported."

"Ain't my decision," Lead Eye said.

"Let's go," Griff said to Jada. "No time left."

"This is crazy," Lu said. "Melia's still in the heights."

"Then you should call her," said Griff.

Lu typed numbers on the 'Link screen as the alphas leapt out and dashed into the Ether Shield. Melia's freckled face appeared moments later.

"Listen," Lu said, "You need to get to the wall district. The Ether Shield's going to disappear any second. Hodge has a stronghold inside the Diamond."

"The wall district?" asked Melia, frowning. "Have you flipped your circuits?"

"Hodge is up there. Take the tram and wait at the transit interval. I'll send someone to get you."

"You're serious?"

"Randy won't forgive me if something happens to you. Just go."

"I'm going," she said. "You'd better be there." Her face dispersed into virtual atoms. Lu turned to me.

"Griff said you could get through the shield. Can you meet Melia on the wall? I'll have to call my rental to pick up me and Lead Eye once the shield goes down."

"Sure," I said. Hopping out the cargo hatch, I approached the Ether Shield. It was barely visible, like heat waves. I'd stowed away on the back of a hunter's RV when I first came to Starlight City. Whoever operated the shield had made a vortex so they could drive through to Nahzir's Gate.

This time, I ran straight through.

The crystal haze was baking my skin off. For the second time, I would die at the hands of something beautiful — or it certainly felt that way. I kept sprinting through the shield, screaming. Finally making it through, I fell to my knees, fists clenched, still screaming as I watched my skin glow and sizzle. The wind felt like splinters of ice. New skin grew over exposed tissue in my hands and arms. The burning became itching, like insects crawling all over me.

I felt the cool wind on my skin as the itching subsided. My clothes had burned away. Taking long, deep breaths, I turned to look at the Ether Shield arching across the sky overhead. From below, it looked like an endless rainbow.

Naked, I climbed the outer wall to the top of the Diamond. All the action of late had suited me nicely. I hardly broke a sweat as I clambered over the edge. The wall surface wasn't paved near the north end and was uninhabited here.

West Four-Nineteen began somewhere along the northwest edge of the Diamond. Unlike my last visit here, the place was abandoned, the housing units empty. No scents lingered on the air.

Everyone had gone below.

At a unit on my right with boarded windows, a diffuse neon sign above me simply read *Bar*. The door hung open with no one inside.

I passed dozens of two-story units with concrete walls of graffiti as I headed toward the gap in the Diamond, which was more of a gape now thanks to Griff.

Hodge's recruits guarded it. I didn't want to explain why I was naked, so instead, I slipped over the wall to sneak by them, climbing up again between two brick units. One was Deacon's. Crates of fruit at the vendors' stands were empty except for a few green melons and an orange in the bottom of one.

Thrift clothing still piled in crates and on shelves beneath awnings. I rummaged through to find a pair of cotton long johns and some faded jeans with frayed cuffs. They were a tad loose, so I tied a string from a pair of combat boots through the belt loops. I found a trench cloak almost like Deacon's, except it was black and had multiple pockets, inside and out. I slipped it on, and the boots as well.

The silver West-8 tram pulled away from the platform as I reached the transit interval. Melia stood near the platform, anxiety in her eyes, her copper hair blowing in the dusty wind.

"Melia?" She faced me. "I'm Black, Lu's boy. Remember me?"

"Where's Lu?" she asked, taking a step toward me.

"I'm supposed meet him."

She followed me to the gape, where recruits with burners still stood guard. They nodded when they recognized me, and we stepped inside the Diamond.

More recruits, some of them quasi-human, were gathered on the top balcony floor. I could tell they were on edge. Several stood guard at the lift further down. One guy with a modified, porcelain face saluted us casually and stepped aside to let us on. He flipped the lever to send us down.

Halogen lights glowed along each balcony rail we passed. On the ground, screens on the Omega generator softly pulsated blue, displaying "No Signal."

Another recruit drove us to the tram station where residents crowded by the tracks. Two trams full of people disappeared through the underground tramway.

I found Hodge at the control box, sliding levers to activate two empty trams. Miles stood beside her, watching her work.

"What's going on?" Melia asked Hodge. "Where's Lu?"

"He's supposed to meet us here," Hodge answered.

"He should be here soon," I told them. "I'll head up in case they need a hand."

I left Melia with Hodge, who started directing residents to the two trams. Gunshots sounded on the surface above. I hurried to the lift as the car descended. Deacon stood alone behind the gate. A Magnum revolver poked from his belt. I gave him the peace-sign salute, a gesture I'd learned as a Soldier of Peace long ago.

"Have you seen the news streams?" he asked. "Kids are headed here on the trams, trying to leave the city. I'd say we offer a hand."

"Let's say," I shrugged, stepping on with him and riding back up. We climbed a ladder to the barrack roof and crawled out the gape. White smoke swirled from a wrecked patrol cruiser that had flipped over near Deacon's unit. A few guards guards lay near it, unconscious. Hodge's recruits looked anxious. Two tended to a wounded ally sitting against the inner fence. Another group walked toward us, escorting several kids to the armory.

We fell in with other recruits heading to the transit interval, posting behind empty crates that once held vendors' merchandise.

Here a full platoon waited anxiously, not saying much, ready for whatever would come. I spotted Lu's air cart overhead, making eye contact with Lead Eye beside him.

The cart whistled to a smooth landing and they stepped off.

Lu tossed me the Zeta .17 he'd bought me. "Is Melia with Hodge?" he asked. I nodded, glancing at Lead Eye.

"So is Miles," I said.

The West-16 pulled to the platform, and more kids got off. Some looked scared as recruits escorted them to the armory. Others seemed excited. I turned toward the vendor's section and saw Griff and Jada walking toward us, pausing once or twice to speak to recruits, or warn them, as they began moving about nervously.

The West-17 arrived; Regime soldiers burst through the doors, weapons hot, catching us off guard. More soldiers rappelled the inside wall, firing and running for cover. Other's raced by on air carts, firing from above.

"Get down," Lu barked. We hit the deck, laying firepower on thick.

A shadow eclipsed the sun overhead, and Coral landed in front of us, right out of the blessed sky. Her sickle arms flared white, and a shockwaves ripped up the concrete. The force sent me rolling backwards as rocks pelted my face. Bigger chunks barely missed my head. The pavement shook beneath me as Coral stood with a smirk on her lips, admiring her destruction.

Bailey landed beside her, cracking the surface. He fired rockets at recruits crouched behind the brick buildings. One exploded near Lead Eye and Deacon, who'd taken cover in front of me. We were blasted with dust and rocks.

Griff whacked his blade arm against Bailey's pulse cannon. Bailey's laugh rang hollow over gunfire – a disturbing laugh. In his grey eyes was a look of insanity, just like the eyes of the Anna II prototype.

More soldiers rushed from the next tram that arrived. Droves climbed the wall like ants. It was full-on war. I instinctively began barking orders, remembering my old comrades and how we died on our first assignment.

"You three, get down below," I yelled, hoping this time I could save my team. I charged the Zeta .17's hyper beam. "Tell Hodge it's turning ugly."

"We're not leaving," said Lu crouched beside me.

"Nobody's waiting for me down below," I yelled back. "So y'all go."

Lu looked at them and back at me, nodded and headed for the armory. The other two followed. I covered their backs, then searched for a vantage point. Recruits and Regime soldiers lay scattered along the Diamond surface, dead or wounded. A second floor window of a brick unit across from me was shattered. I raced for the unit door, and shrapnel ripped through my right forearm. I dropped the photon burner, doubling over in pain. My cells regenerated faster than ever, and the wounds were sealed.

After almost hyperventilating, I grabbed the burner and pumped a shrapnel round at the keypad lock, kicked the door open and tripped running up the creaky stairs. In the empty room upstairs, the walls had chipped green paint. Looking through the broken window, I charged the hyper burst. Bailey shielded Griff's onslaught with his cannon. Coral's sickle arms flared, blasting Griff from behind and forcing him into Bailey, who clamped his metal claw around Griff's face. The crushing pressure dented his jaw and shorted out the glow of his right eye.

Griff fought free as Jada's grenade went off in Bailey's face, shredding the skin off one side. With part of his lips gone, he looked to be grinning, touching his fingers to the chromium jaw beneath.

Bailey shielded a second grenade with his cannon barrel. Griff was on Coral's heels. He forced her near the building where I was crouched at the window. I aimed and fired; the hyper beam hit with a flash of light, making sparks shoot off her shoulder, but was mostly absorbed. She froze, and Griff slammed into her, whipping his blade arms with a timely spark that blew pieces off her left sickle arm.

Griff charged again but she slipped away, swinging her other arm chaotically, slamming it to the surface with such force that it shook the building's whole foundation. The floor collapsed and I fell through. Trapped under debris, I tried digging my way out while explosions shook the world all about me. My leg was stuck under an aluminum slab weighted down by bricks. I had to slide my leg while pulling the slab with it.

It took forever to crawl from the darkness. The violent quaking had ceased when I finally saw the sunlight. Griff sat in silence with his back against a toppled brick wall. He was hardly recognizable with his exterior so mangled and parts of his frame exposed. He stared at Jada on the ground beside him, lying motionless, arms spread. Coral had collapsed not far off, and Bailey lay face down nearby. They were all mangled. I stood, walking toward Griff.

"What happened?" I asked. Griff looked up. His one glowing eye stared in bewilderment.

"They just – Nahzir just fried their circuits."

E-Streams Extracted
Log-013..

    Michelle came to see me again, but it's only Thor's Day. She snuck in with some New Testament activists scheduled for a tour of the prison. She opened the bible she held to give me a small jump drive that was inside. She'd copied audio files from the ROM in Griffin's ThinkCap© sitting on my desk but can't make sense of them. I asked her about Griffin. Nothing. That was her reply. The StarMack was still connected. The Anna III model was still in the storage cabinet, but Griffin was gone.

    So that's it then. It's all over.

    I'm still holding the recorder she gave me. I should listen to it and stop being a coward.......

Thomas Hurst -- NewStream Daily

Chapter 15

Surviving recruits crawled from hiding. Regime soldiers still alive had abandoned post during the alpha's battle. Stillness lingered now. The city's sounds could barely be heard. Griff watched the sky with one glowing eye, and I heard a whistling sound moving closer, until an elliptical halo craft descended from the clear blue sky. Bright lights encircled its girth like Saturn's rings.

"*Nahzir.*"

I jumped at the sound of Griff's loud, hollow voice. He stood. The halo craft hovered in place as whoever was inside watched us through the dark convex window. My hairs stood on end.

The halo craft reflexively rose as Griff moon-jumped, shock-blade arms drawn. He pierced the craft's exterior as he slammed against it. The craft sank toward the Diamond further from where I stood, rocking back and forth. Griff clawed his way toward the window at the center. The rings spun faster with a flashing light. There was an ear-splitting, ringing sound, and a gust of wind blew off my hood. The wind picked up like a cyclone. I crouched behind a broken wall and saw a blinding flash. Griff was flung from the craft and across the surface, smashing through brick unit after brick unit, tumbling halfway across the vendors' section.

I raced to where he lay still on the ground. The framework in his left leg was exposed; so was his right calf. The hydraulic spring in his ankle he used to moon-jump had snapped. He sat up, his auburn face covered with dirt. His teeth were clenched as he held one mech arm in front of him. Sparks shot from the shock-blade hanging limply from his chromium arm like a broken wing.

Slowly, he stood. With his other arm, he grabbed his broken blade at the base and snapped it off, releasing a hollow grunt. He held the blade in his hand, glaring at the ascending halo craft getting smaller and smaller. Soon, it was only a speck.

"To the next planet he can infest," uttered Griff. "He took our flesh bodies. I saw them inside."

Returning to where Jada lay still, he stood over her. My heart wrenched when he started hammering his Shock-blade against the side of her face. Thinking his circuits had flipped, I started to grab his shoulder but was afraid to stop him. I could only watch, speechless, as he cracked her face open. He knelt down, unhinged the silvery skull and reached a hand inside, trying to work something free. He tore out a glowing electronic device with a gelatinous membrane and popped the small jump drive from behind his ear. He peeled away the membrane, plugging the jump drive into the device. The glow of the device faded, and the circuitry inside the jump drive glowed bright.

"Stay here if you want," Griff said, standing and replacing the jump drive behind his ear. He looked at the colorful building screens through the fence. Several displayed Regime soldiers fighting creatures that had found their way into the city. "I've had my fill of this place."

Children and battle-worn recruits sat quietly beside the tracks at the station below, waiting for the trams to return. We smoked cigars until hazy rays of the evening sun shone through the gape above. The fragrant smoke made my lungs feel alive, like I could run fifty miles nonstop. Griff said it was my regenerative cells using the nitrosamines for fuel. I asked if he could feel or taste it. He wasn't sure, but he liked how a strong puff made white noise flicker across his vision.

Just after sundown, a rickety tram squealed from the tunnel. Sleeping kids began to rise. Beside me, two sleepy sisters, curled in blankets and jackets they borrowed from recruits, stood up and yawned. The taller one carried a fluffy animal backpack. The little sister rubbed her tired eyes as they boarded the front car. We let others get on first and boarded the third car as another tram pulled in. Recruits boarded this last tram while ours started into the underground tramway.

Through the window behind Griff were elaborate etchings on the tunnel wall. Graffiti art. Once the tram picked up speed, I only saw the art in glimpses, like flashing holo ads.

They stretched on for miles.

Leaning against the window behind me, I watched the markings for at least a rev before closing my eyes. I might have dozed a little. When I opened them again, Griff was like a statue with an empty stare. His body seemed vacant, like his conscious mind had drifted elsewhere. I'd never seen his eyes not analyzing something.

After a while, he became aware again and saw me staring.

"Dreaming?" I asked. He nodded.

"Connecting to Jada," he answered. "Her C-conscious was visiting one of our memories."

♦

Someone Else

"This is supposed to be Starlight City," Griff said to Jada. "There's nothing here." He looked up the grassy hillside along dense forest where they'd just been extracted. The halo craft that dropped them off was returning to the Zenith. "Did they give us the right coordinates?"

"Apparently not," answered Jada after a moment's pause. "My GPS says it's ninety kilometers east of here." The pupil in her left eye dilated as she widened her display of a satellite map only she could see. Griff found it curious how one pupil was wider than the other. Viewing the world from the eye in the sky, she seemed adrift in a far-off place.

A gray blur sprung from the trees behind her. Griff dashed, his mecha arm drawn. His Shock-blade hacked through a thick neck. The head flipped, and the body thudded heavily into the soft dirt. Griff glared at the head looking up at him with snarling teeth. The species registered in his retinal scanner – a double-muscle hellhound. He'd seen them on the weekly "Hunter's Bulletin" news feeds. The rage was leaving its eyes like a flame extinguished.

More mutant hounds bolted down the hillside. Jada's Hexgun

snapped open, popping shrapnel that ripped through mounds of thick muscle. Two of the beasts collapsed. A third lunged for her. Planting her feet, she rammed with her shoulder, recoiling from the force as the hound staggered on hind legs. Jada closed the space, thrusting the Hexgun harpoon into the beast's underbelly. A yelp escaped its jaws. Jada ripped the harpoon free, smashing her gun against its skull. The beast toppled sidelong, skidding across the grass. It stood again, panting heavily, desperation in its eyes. Two shrapnel bursts quickly ended its misery.

"Look sharp," Jada said calmly. "Multiple blips on the scanner. They're coming from everywhere."

A swarm raced down the hillside; more flooded from the woods in packs. Griff went into overdrive, both shock-blades spinning with calculate precision. He moved at inhuman speeds, dodging the swift beasts snapping their strong jaws shut millimeters from his neck. One after another, he laid waste to them, until few near him were left alive. Those fled into the woods, but Griff could sense them still lurking.

He stood in a meadow near the hillside, the felled beasts surrounding him. The grass here was dark green and rather plush.

Across the meadow was a river with trees lining the opposite bank. A narrow waterfall spilled over pearl rocks of an adjacent cliff above.

Jada walked toward him. Smoke swirled from the Hexgun extension she'd used. Three shrapnel clips dropped from her outstretched arm, clattering in the grass. Griff heard her shoulder flap open as more clips slid into position. He heard it click shut, snapping them in place. Jada aimed to his left, spurting more shrapnel. Sparks and emptied casings sprayed from her shoulder with sounds like ringing steel.

She ceased fire. The living silence of the Forests resonated. The carnage they'd dealt seemed unreal, like it happened in a dream, or some alternate existence. But the evidence of their destruction was there – the bodies lying still in the grass, the dark blood on Griff's shock-blades and the mecha arms that wielded them. The same dark blood speckled Jada's face and the sleek uniform fitted to her feminine frame.

"There's something they didn't mention," Griff said.

"It's some kind of test, logically," said Jada. She walked toward the swift flowing water of the shallow river, her weapon hidden now, and her arm a human's arm again.

"Nahzir and his demented tests." Griff retracted his mecha arms with several clacks. His forearm snapped onto his elbow again. He moved to the water's edge, watching her wade into the flowing stream with most of her thighs covered.

"What are you doing?" he asked her.

"We can't be covered in hellhound blood in Starlight City. We should wash it off."

"True. Can't have city walkers thinking we're savages. Bad first impression." He followed her in as she cut against the current toward the waterfall. She walked beneath it, and the water cascaded over her face, rinsing blood and grime from her long, pitch-black hair. She swept her hands over her face and brushed her uniform, scrubbing away death's stains, and turned to face Griff again. Water glistened on her olive skin. Griff thought he felt a vague sense of longing. It was gone before he could grasp what it was.

"Your turn," she said. Griff waded past her. His skin felt cool beneath the flowing water, his body alive with sensation. He opened his eyes wide and let the water pour into them as it washed through his short, silver hair. He felt Jada's slender fingers running across his shoulders and down his back, wiping blood away.

"Hard to wash it from the nylon in your uniform," she said. "It rinses off the steel." Griff faced Jada, blinking twice to clear water from his lenses. His vision was crystal clear. Jada's eyes were glowing. Behind her violet irises, beneath small numbers etched there, he saw ultra-white rings of light.

They bolted across lush terrain of the Forests at blinding speed, Griff closely tailing Jada, who navigated with her internal GPS, moving headlong for Starlight City. They crossed miles of the exotic landscape where trees flourished and myriad colorful plants grew wild. Griff's retinal scanner recognized plant and animal species stored in his C-conscious. Jada ignored the heat signals racing at them from different directions, creatures of the Forests, seemingly drawn to their energy.

In less than two revs, they reached the Ether Shield, a faint orange grid in Griff's vision. Jada stuck a slim arm into the shield. The orange light faded around it.

Creatures behind them gathered in numbers but kept their distance. Ignoring them, Griff followed Jada into the shield. The intense energy coursed through his circuitry, merging with the energy inside him. The bounds of this energy felt limitless.

Some of the creatures darted into the shield after them, shrieking and howling as the energy seared them into dissipating mist. Griff watched over his shoulder as they became mere ghosts of light, quickly fading.

Cloudscrapers behind the city wall stretched toward the sky.

"We're at the west end," said Jada. "Nahzir's Gate is on the east."

Griff was looking up the wall. He bent his knees and moon-jumped. The blast from his heels vaulted him over the wall's edge high above. He landed heavily on the surface amidst a crowd of startled wanderers. Jada landed beside him.

"There's a SkyTram station right around this bend, behind those units." Griff motioned toward brick houses ahead. Ivy grew over the mortar of the one beside them.

"That's affirmed," said Jada. "How could you know that? This is our first time here."

"I lived in this city once. Remember how I said we all had flesh bodies?"

"I know what you said," she replied. "It's illogical. Our minds were designed from simulated brain data. We're not the people whose brain data was copied. That's not how it works."

Griff could see the transit station beyond the crowded vendor's section where a man on the end sold bottled water from stacked cases. The West-17 sat idle on the track as anxious passengers filed into its open doors. Near the fence along the wall, a man in jeans and a gray hood cloak preached aloud on a wooden crate, his back to the brilliant city.

"But we shall all be changed," Griff heard the man say over the noise of bargainers. He was ignored by most of the passersby, but a few wanderers had gathered near to listen intently.

"I could show you how to get to any landmark in this city," Griff said to Jada. "How do you explain that?" He wanted to tell her everything.

"It isn't plausible," she said after a pause, "Unless you —"

"Hurst copied my memory," Griff confessed. "I'm the same person from before."

Jada stopped.

"Hurst said we were all blank slates," she muttered. "Why

would he give you memories?"

"Nahzir let him do it."

"But those are unstable parameters," she argued. "Besides, even with those memories, you're still not that person." Her voice raised in pitch.

Griff stopped ahead of her at the crowded tram interval. The realization socked him hard. Jada was right. He wasn't the same person at all. He was someone else entirely. Everything about him was artificial. His sensations were programmed. He couldn't remember what it was to actually "feel" anything inside. Between human awareness and his mechanized body, there was a disconnection, something lost in transmission – something he vaguely remembered as human.

They stepped on the crowded tram and raced toward the skyline.

Back at the Zenith, in the Alpha Bunker below ground, it was time to dream.

Griff's head was connected to the brain wave scatterer in his quarters beside Bailey, his bunkmate. With their brains connected to the same CyberNet domains, the alphas could drift into each other's dreams.

Conscious streams raced through his C-Conscious at random, interspersing his past and the present. He remembered joys of childhood, love, the sorrow of loss. In his dreams, he felt these things. He was full of emotions. He unplugged himself from the module, trying to retain these feelings. But in waking moments, his mind grasped only concepts. The magic of his dreams was intangible.

Perturbed, he rose from his rest module, exited the room and walked the length of the corridor. He took the lift up to the surface, stepped out the bunker door and was met by a whirlwind of snow. He felt cold sensation as blankets of white blew against him, but no discomfort, just a shift in temperature.

He trekked through the blizzard down the mountainside, his mind racing. As much as he hated being a hand tool of Nahzir's Regime, the emptiness he now felt was much worse.

Through the white snow, he saw the green and orange lights streamlining the railcar at the stop below.

He stepped into the dimly lit car. The whiteness of the storm outside made the world seem empty. He was alone in the universe, except for his reflection. He pushed the manual control and the car shoved off. Again, he stared at the face in the glass. It was like the face he'd always known, but wasn't quite the same.

"Hi, I'm nobody," it said to him.

Approaching the Neuron Research Compound, he flipped the stop lever.

At the compound, Griff walked in from the storm, tracking snow on the plush, synthetic floor of the main lobby. It was empty; the wall screens were dark. Workers had retired to their quarters on upper floors for the night.

Beyond the lobby, Griff took the lift to level sixty-three. At the end of the hall, he stopped at Hurst's door. He'd thought Hurst might shed some light – help him fill the empty void. He raised a hand to knock, hesitant.

Hurst couldn't change anything, Griff thought. He hardly even saw himself as Hurst's son. He was a manifestation of Hurst and Nahzir's limitless imaginations, just like the other alphas.

Unsettled, he moved on, turned the corner and accessed the Unit C throughway. Passing through a second door, he stopped near the opposite hallway in front of the Unit C workroom where he'd been reborn just three cycles prior.

Biology session was the last time he'd been here, five days ago. He had downloaded the Rebirth Project data to his CyberNet brain. Nahzir wanted the alphas to compose a document explaining why all but one of the experiments had failed. No one could figure it out.

The round door opened as Griff stepped toward it. He saw the holo of the shotgun blade arm Hurst designed, rotating on the StarMack interface. It was just like a toy he'd had as a kid. He popped the jump drive from behind his ear and hooked it to the interface, downloading the designs to his memory, a keepsake.

Griff walked the curving stairs to the workroom's lower level. The modified humans, supposedly dormant, floated in containment cells along the back wall. Like him, they'd been human once, had died, and now were something else entirely – all except the one.

He hopped on the ledge and stood in front of cell seven. Unlike the other specimens, this one was unmistakably human. Whatever modifications it had undergone, the evidence wasn't visible.

The man floated, unconscious, breathing through a tube strapped to his steel muzzle. As Griff watched, the eyes slowly opened, and he saw the evidence. They weren't human eyes. They were a lambent, amber hue, with black pupils widening and constricting.

Before he knew what was happening, Griff had extended his right mecha arm, charged his shock-blade and sliced a gash through the fiberglass. The blade sparked bright as the glowing Hydra Resin fluid inside sloshed out. With more strikes, he mutilated the glass and watched the body slide onto the white lab floor. The specimen twitched in spasms.

Griff rammed into the next cell headfirst, denting the fiberglass and leaving thousands of intricate cracks. Drawing his other Shock-blade, he swung both at full charge. Fluid exploded from the shattering cell.

He destroyed the other cells, releasing the dormant specimens. Streams of fluid gushed onto the floor as Griff exited the round door, stalking through the hallway beyond the workroom. Alarms screamed, and a soldier peeked warily from a room down the hall. The soldier pointed, yelling, "He's flipped," running off to alert others. Griff ignored, hurling himself through a hall window. His knee shattered concrete sixty-three floors below, and he broke into full sprint up a steep incline behind the compound.

Not once did he look back. He would get as far away as possible – not because he was afraid. He needed to leave his false existence – leave it all behind. He would venture far into the Forests, into the unknown. To himself, he was something unknown. His only hope was that in uncovering the strange world without, he might discover something of his new self – something tangible he could embrace.

E-Streams Extracted
Log-014..

    I decided to address the public, knowing the audio file from Griffin's ThinkCap© would have an impact. Regime officials were there, and Administer Nahzir himself arranged to meet with me here in the penthouse chamber of Denizen's Hall. It seems they weren't trying to silence me. They really did consider me dangerous, but they had no clue what I was working on.

    The guard who escorted me here says Nahzir's fascinated by my work. He doesn't know the details but says Nahzir's been working on a project, an army of ultra-intelligent, humanoid war machines. He insists that if I work with Nahzir, he'll let me bring Griffin back as part of the project. Can I trust him? Who knows what he's after?

    Looks like I'll need a plan Z. Maybe I'll upload my conscious data onto the StarMack and disappear into the CyberNet®. Griffin's in there somewhere – maybe Anna too. There must be a way I can find them. A street poet near the dawn of this millennium once asked, "Why should we die to go to heaven? Earth is already in space." Wishful dreaming, maybe.......

Thomas Hurst -- NewStream Daily

Lee

Chapter 16

It took almost a full thirty-two revs to travel through the underground tramway. Sunlight blinded me as the tram slowed. My eyes quickly focused. "We're at some kind of station," I said, looking over at Griff. His eyes were blank again, and with his battered frame, it looked like he could have been dead. The door opened, and recruits stepped off. The few kids in our car were asleep.

Feeling an urge to stretch my legs and take a leak, I walked out the doors onto a rusted platform. The operator was near the front car, dragging thick cords from a large, peculiar apparatus inside a fence.

Thorny shrubs grew to the platform's edge in front of a grass-splotched valley. Toward the rear of the tram were weathered, moss-covered sculptures with wings. Grim faces were carved into them. One severed stone wing lay in the grass nearby.

I stepped into the harsh foliage, relieving myself as I looked across the warped terrain. In the distance on far off hills, the sparse vegetation ceased, like someone had drawn a border for it. On the other side was nothing but white sand. Right at the border, I saw a broken bridge reaching above nearby trees. It was tilted backwards, as if being swallowed by the earth.

"The edge of where the Life Bomb hit," I heard Griff say beside me.

Starlight City

"Jeez, kid," I jumped. "You always sneak up on people? Trying to piss if you don't mind."

"I wonder how much of Neon was white desert before all this," he said, as if he hadn't heard me

The operator rallied us up after recharging the engine, and the tram pushed on.

For half the day, we crossed the crater-filled desert plains.

In the gray of night, we approached moving lights on the horizon. Coming closer, I saw they were round solar panels on windmill blades spinning on rooftops of small houses. The track curved the edge of this quaint town before cutting through. Residents in heavy coats stood near homes with lit windows. The tram slowed, cruising past more houses where children ran through the white sand between.

Beyond houses at the edge of the cold desert town, a strange copper glow shined from the ground. The tram stopped near the edge of town. Stepping off, we stood close enough to see a vast crater surrounding the copper light. We spotted Hodge among recruits outside the empty houses.

"Boss lady," our tram operant said, approaching Hodge as the last tram pulled in behind ours. "We're the last to cross the dessert."

Hodge nodded. "Tell the folks not to stray too far from town," she said. "Haven't seen nothing dangerous, but who knows." She turned to us for the first time, staring open-mouthed at Griff. "You look like hell," she mumbled.

"I feel marvelous," Griff replied dryly. It was hard to tell if he was joking or serious.

"Come on, Black." Hodge walked toward the crater, pointing toward the light. "Take a look."

We approached the rim of the crater, and I saw the massive starship. The girth of it filled the crater. Its shiny exterior, streamlined with copper-tone lights, reflected the amber moon above.

"There she is," Hodge said. "Your pal Griff powered the Omega engines. Took three revs to get it full up and running."

"Who would leave behind a starship?" I wondered.

"Same ones who built the Diamond and never turned on the generators," said Hodge. "That'd be my guess, anyway. Whoever they were, I wish they were here. I'd kiss them."

She led us behind a house along the track. Miles was sitting beside Lead Eye on a rock near a fire pit, holding a thorny stick to the flame. Deacon sat in the sand across from them, with Naudica sleeping against his arm and Augie curled at her feet. The wolf licked his lips, staring at Lu, who poked at a juicy piece of meat roasting in a skillet over the fire. The look of shock on their faces when they saw Griff was sort of funny. Melia covered her mouth with her hand.

"Where's Jada?" Lu asked, breaking the awkward silence.

"Nahzir fried her wiring," said Griff. "But she's here in spirit."

We stared quietly at the crackling flames.

"Will mom's spirit meet us in the next world?" Miles asked Lead Eye. I noticed the scar on his temple, a symbol of Jada's human soul.

"She's already waiting for us," said Deacon.

"What happened to her?" I asked.

"Hopefully putting her in that preservatory on the ship will keep her cells are in a cryogenic state," said Lead Eye.

Silence followed again. Lu took the sizzling meat from the skillet, placing it in a foil pan on a table beside the fire.

"I just remembered something," I said, reminded by the mention of cells. "Nahzir said my cells could cure diseases. You don't suppose – "

"He actually told you that?" asked Griff. "The chances of a human body accepting your cells without gross mutation are nonexistent. He never even knew why yours accepted them. One of our research assignments was to study your reanimation and explain how it occurred. No one figured it out."

"Seems you've found favor with God, Black," said Deacon, smiling.

Griff turned to Miles. "It's theoretically possible to track C-conscious data streaming in timeless space." he said. "We'll catch your mom somewhere – and mine. We'll warp through the multiverse if we have to."

The starship had satellite access, and we could pick up Starlight City news feeds with our 'Links. The most popular streams reported that wall residents had mysteriously vanished with the Ether Shield.

After Nahzir "Abandoned this world," as the news phrased it, Regime Soldiers returned from the Zenith to protect their homes. They swept the streets, hunting down hostile creatures that had broken through Nahzir's Gate. They set up a firewall outside of the gate, thwarting attempts of other savage creatures trying to break through.

They handled this without much trouble. The real concern was the aggressive microorganisms the shield kept out. Several people got sick, and a few died. The others were treated with Hydra Resin injections at health clinics. No one else was affected.

People speculated about why.

Then, classified research reports went public, documenting that the surrounding ecosystem Nahzir's Life Bomb created had shown signs of stabilizing over the last five cycles. Many known mutant bacterial strands had disappeared. Nahzir had kept this from the public.

Months passed with no further reports. Recruits thought the city would fall into chaos. Seems they were wrong.

We all lived in "Windmill Town," as we started calling it, for almost a full cycle before Griff and some of the crew decided upon setting the starship on course for Earth. He said that's where Nahzir would go. He wanted to track him down and get his body back. We all left Neon except for Lu, who said he'd never stop looking for his friend Randy. At least a third of the West Four Nineteen residents, mostly kids, moved into the quarters on the ship.

Griff found raw materials stockpiled on the ship that he used to repair his body, plus Hodge is helping him build the shotgun blade-arm his father designed. He's set up NewStream accounts for his parents too, and Miles's mom, for when he tracks their subconscious data. He'll store them in his CyberNet brain and upload them to their NewStream feeds. When I asked how he'd find them, he said he'd follow the voice in his head.

Sometimes, he seems a little insane — but who's to say what's sane in an infinitely expanding universe, or what's possible, for that matter? I died once; now, I'm alive again, and I'm living on this starship. It blows my mind. Makes me think of that old saying, "All dogs go to heaven." Apparently, it applies to old dogs too.

It seems I'm at the end of this media stream. I'll close with another stream Griff played for me, proof of his own "rebirth."

It's mystifying.

"When I died," Griff told me, "My consciousness began to rise. Neon's forests and vast mountain ranges were indescribably beautiful. The oceans were intense blues. I ascended into space, beyond our two moons, Amber and Pearl, drifting for what seemed like years."

He went on, "Dad thought he was copying my subconscious with the neuron mapper he found in that Stargazer, not realizing the subconscious is part of the soul, and you can't copy souls." He paused.

"Or as Deacon would say," he went on, "We can't outdo God. Copying my subconscious data just opened a fourth-dimensional warp, and my soul got sucked through it."

He popped the silver jump drive from his ear. "This was his last journal log. He attached an audio file recorded from my old ThinkCap."

♦

"It's zero two-hundred, regulation time. I'm coming home from school. Feeling a little sick. Head's killing me. Maybe this ThinkCap's on too tight. I take a pain capsule and turn on my 'Link to work on the design for our grad project. Can hardly see anything. Must be a migraine. That tall girl Jaden from Cosmology session walks through our kitchen. No, we're in the cafeteria. She sees me watching her and comes to sit. I ask if she wants to go uptown some night. She smiles.

We're in the Argyle Mountains; they're just like I imagined from the holos. Jaden's sliding down a cliff, the same way mom did in my dream when she grew wings. I wonder if Jaden has wings.

She looks afraid. I catch her hand as she falls. When I pull her up, she's light as air. Standing on solid ground again. She wraps her arms around me. We kiss. Am I imagining this?

Must have been. I'm in my room. Head still hurts, but my vision's clear. Something's weird. So much color, like paintballs exploding inside a Zero-G vacuum. I reach out to touch it and my fingers look like brown spiders. I can't feel the color; it's just light.

Someone's face is at the window outside. It's glowing like the colors. I go to the window, retracting the blinds.

Mom?

It's her, looking in at me. It's cold outside, so I go to the door and see why she doesn't come in. Where is she? The sun hides behind the pinkest cloud. Threads of color drift through the air. I come back inside, and Mom's there when I close the door. She's trying to say something but has no voice...

She's down the hall, staring at the basement door. I follow her into Dad's lab. She's standing by his Alchemy table, looking at a sealed jar with a caution label. She points at the jar. No, she's vanished. Inside the jar? I open it and peek inside. An odd smell gets in my nose, like burned licorice. I can't breathe. Color spilling everywhere. The colors are white, and Mom is floating up.

I'm in the lab again, sitting at Dad's Alchemy station. Something in the jar oozes out. My face is lying in it. I feel myself floating, except it can't be me because I'm still lying there.

I see our house and all of Gallagher Heights below.

Soaring above cloudscrapers.

Stars swirl above like a vortex – or am I spinning? Some stars have faces, the faces of angels, circling around me, faster and faster, a perfect circle . . . (brain wave signal lost)

NewStream Daily

Chapter 17

We spent months on the mothership. I stayed in contact with Lu on my 'Link to see how long the connection would last. When we finally left the darkness of the Sequiter and appeared in the starlit Milky Way, I was shocked to hear Lu's voice."

"Black? You still there?"

"Holy holiday," I couldn't help but say. So the CyberNet could span across galaxies.

There hadn't been much to do with all that time besides surf the Net on StarMack consoles in the ship lobbies, which we all did for hours on end. I started this NewStream account and posted *Starlight City* on the Net, trying to spread the word about Nahzir, hoping someone could lead us to him.

Days after reaching the Milky Way, we approached Harmonica, the floating, metallic city with bright lights inside a glass-like sphere. Earth looked massive through the bridge floor below us, like we could land on the clouds.

A transmission came through the ship monitors.

This is Harmonica Port City. Please identify yourself.

"My name is Thomas Hurst," said Griff. "I'm a Biotech scientist from the planet Neon." He saw me eyeing him strangely. "This might draw out the real Tom Hurst, if he's here," he told me quietly.

"I'm Black Freemont," I told the voice.

"State your intentions," the voice demanded.

"We're pursuing a criminal from named Nahzir," said Griff. "He's a danger to your planet."

"Hold it. Records say Captain Black Freemont died over a decade ago. You trying to get over on me?"

"Maybe it was another Black Freemont," I blurted.

"Sure, I guess. But your ship is too large to land here. You'll have to go Earth-side. Talk to the people in charge there. I'm sending you classified coordinates to a spaceport which will be erased upon docking. I must warn you that the surrounding area is uncharted for international security purposes. You'll have find your way down there."

"Can't we land on the moon?" Griff asked.

"Negative. Politicians have forbidden any ship to go on or off the moon."

"You can't raise the restraint for international security?" Griff persisted. "We believe Nahzir may have gone to the moon."

"Not possible. Everyone goes Earth-side. This is the military. We don't intervene in politics, so please redirect your ship."

Griff shut off the transmission and changed course. "We're wasting time trying to argue with a computer," he said. "Earth-side it is."

"Why would Nahzir go to the moon?" I asked.

"That's where he was born. There was no livable atmosphere there before his old man tested the first Life Bomb. His father's considered the pioneer of off-world civilization." He turned to me. "But we know that's a lie."

As we dropped into Earth's mesosphere, flames outside the ship began to fade. I could see for miles beneath clouds. Swiftly descending toward the planet surface, we looked across the vast terrain, all tundra with pockets of snow.

We landed at the spaceport and stepped into an empty hangar. No one worked inside the spaceport except small, wheeled robots that ran calculations on the electronic equipment all day. It was decided Griff and I would check things out while the others stayed with the ship. Green arrows marked the path to the designated exit. All other routes were blocked. We followed the path through a maze that led to an elevator, which swiftly took us down. The doors opened to snow-covered fields. We looked up. The spaceport was anchored high above a man-made, concrete ravine by massive steel beams. The only entrance was the elevator. It had a lock keypad on the doors, which had already closed.

An ancient steam locomotive sat idle at an old train station ahead of us. A display screen near the track flashed "Please Enter." We stepped into a passenger car, and the train started up loudly. The engines whistled, and the train pulled off, taking us far into the countryside. I tried to remember train rides as a kid, but could only think of old movies with train rides.

When we stepped off the train, it started off on its own, back the way we came. We set out on foot across fields of powder-soft snow, hiking for hours along a slightly worn path. Eventually, we reached a public park. Stone seats surrounded a tall clock with a bronze phoenix perched on top. Griff paused. The clock was operating and pointed at 8:00 pm. My instinct felt it was about right.

"If I focus my C-conscious on her Net domain," said Griff. "I think I can download Jada's GPS function and synch to the nearest satellite receiver." He gazed into space. Brushing snow off the closest bench with my trench cloak sleeve, I pulled out a smoke and sat down. A black squirrel jumped onto the arm of the bench beside me, jumped to the ground, snatched an acorn half buried in the soft snow and darted up a tree encircled by the benches. Skimming the bare limbs up top, it leapt to branches of the woods surrounding us.

I waited, smoking half the cigar and feeling ptetty hazy. The woods were silent, except for an owl here or there.

"There's a signal to the east," Griff told me. "Looks like multiple receivers. We should head that way." As I stood to leave, my ears pricked to the sound of metal. We spun quickly to see four bipedal robots with guns for arms marching toward us.

"Pardon," said a male voice meshed with static. "Why are you outside your neighborhood? It's well past curfew."

"Curfew?" I said, shocked. "Are you serious?" I glanced at Griff. Had robots taken over?

"It is advised that you return to your neighborhood," said one, stepping forward. "This park is not open after dark."

Starlight City

Another robot was scanning Griff.

"You are not an organic life form. Analysis shows your life source is gravity and solar energy. You're not authorized to enter the town, but we'll gladly escort you to the nearest factory."

"You mindless glitch," said Griff. "I'll go where I go." They turned weapons on Griff. I drew the photon burner and blew one of them to pieces with a few pulse rounds. Griff ejected his new shotgun blade arms, severing two robots cleanly at the torso as I fried the last one. It collapsed and shorted out in the snow.

"What's going on?" I wondered out loud, looking around for more robots.

"Don't know," said Griff. "Let's head for those receivers."

We moved eastward through the silent woods until we hit a narrow road with cracked pavement, which led us to a small town. The little houses had faded paint and worn siding, and the roofs were in need of repair. They were tightly packed together, and every house had a satellite dish on the roof or in the small, squared lawn.

We reached the town's main road where cars were parked along the curbs. A few sat in the middle of the street. All of them were rusted. We saw a man on a Segway buzz past along the otherwise empty street.

"They must have run out of gas," I speculated. "Or it got too expensive."

A lone woman was passing on the walk. She wore brown lipstick and a long leather coat.

"Excuse me, ma'am," I said. "We're looking for a place to stay."

"No ingles," she said.

"Donde podemos descansar para la noche?" uttered Griff. She looked slightly annoyed.

"Eh, vas adelante de tres calles," she pointed. "Hay un hotel a la izquierda."

"Gracias," I added. She forced a smile and walked on.

I glanced at Griff "Hablas español?" I asked,

"Downloaded several languages," he replied. "Linguistic diversity is high in this area, according to the Net."

A few blocks down, we entered the hotel next to a coffee shop. Inside, and man in a ball cap with leather flaps stood behind the counter.

"Y'all ain't from 'round this way," the man said, squinting at us. "How'd you get by them robots? They don't let out-of-towners in after curfew."

"Had to get physical," said Griff.

"What's with those robots anyway?" I asked the man. "What's going on?"

"It's the politicians," the man replied. "They all went to the moon, and they wired the technology to harvest profit on our labor. Ain't that a bitch?" He banged on the counter, knocking a couple pens on the floor. "And the restricted all Network traffic. Major service providers sold all their customers out."

"Has this happened elsewhere?" Griff wondered.

"For all we know, the robots have taken over the country," the man said. "But how can you really know? Can't leave the town except to trade wares, and they regulate that too. Maybe they took over the world."

"We'd like a room," I said, not entertaining the thought.

"Sure. You got money, right?"

"Money?" I said. "No." The man frowned.

"Anything of value?"

"How about this 'Link device," I took the 'Link from my ear. "It'll let you connect to Net space anywhere, on or off the planet's network."

"Not possible," he said.

"Take it." I laid it on the table. "Just let us have a room key. If you're not happy with it, you can come kick us out. By the way, I'll need it back when we leave."

The man looked skeptical but gave us a key. We walked to the room on the second floor. There were twin beds with clouds sewn on the blue comforters.

"Let's wait and see if the robots come looking for us," said Griff. I was exhausted after travelling from another galaxy through a wormhole, taking a four-hour train ride and walking for nearly ten miles. I plopped onto the bed and went to dreamland.

Hours later, I rose to find Griff standing on the balcony, staring at the sky. It was cold, and I could see steam coming from vents on the shoulder armor he and Hodge built.

"I've linked to a satellite orbiting above," he said. "I've got GPS data on this entire region."

"Good to hear," I said, finding it ironic how this was my home planet and I had no clue where we were.

"Let's track the source of those robots," he insisted. "They seem to have functioning AI's, but I think someone's logging on and using them as avatars too." He walked back inside.

"There's a big factory east of here in a place called The Dakotas. I need to get there. It's best if you stay here. You can't cover ground as quickly as me."

Late that night, the tube ran a remake of Kill Bill in 3D. The woman playing The Bride had lost an arm and had a metal one grafted in its place. I thought about Lead Eye, wondering how old the movie was.

Once it was over, the network ran a bunch of infomercials for cosmetics. There was a knock at the door. Griff and I exchanged glances. I got up and checked the peephole. It was the hotel manager with the leather hat. I let him in.

"Hey, sorry guys, but I need you out, he said. "Robots was here looking for you. I told them I hadn't seen no one, but now you've got to go."

"Not a problem," I said. "Thanks. I'll need my 'Link back."

"Oh. Hey, about that – I'll give you a thousands bucks for this thing. Straight cash, man."

"Done," I said. I didn't need the 'Link as long as I was with Griff, and the cash might come in handy. The manager gave me a pouch full of engraved gold coins.

"Count it if you like," he said. "It's all there."

♦

Rex sat at his computer monitor, staring at a black screen. He'd just watched the battery die, was too tired to get up and plug it in. The harvest this season was more than generous; they'd worked past nightfall.

He may have dozed a while, then heard a voice in his head say *open your eyes*. He saw his screen lit up again and thought he was dreaming. There was a message in his NewStream chat box from a

Tom217.

"Good day."

Rex couldn't think of who it was.

"?" he sent in reply.

"I'm looking for someone who builds robots," said Tom217. "Could you assist me?"

Rex thought it might be a CyberNet surfer pulling a prank, or worse, some kind of criminal, or a maniac. One couldn't tell who was on the other end of the stream.

"Who are you?" Rex typed back.

"My name is Tom Hurst. I'm not sure how this will sound, but I have to find a way out of your computer."

"This a joke?"

"Afraid not. Try to shut off your power." After thinking on it, Rex flipped the power switch on the small hard drive plugged into his twelve-inch laptop monitor. The screen flickered and returned to normal. He tried it again, getting the same result.

"Still here," said Tom.

Rex sat up, sweeping back his dreads, then rubbed his eyes and looked around. He wasn't dreaming. His computer was actually talking to him.

"What do you want from me?" Rex keyed.

"Do you know anyone who constructs robots?"

"Not anyone I know. I don't associate with scientists."

"Engineers, you mean," Tom corrected. "What kind of work do you do, Rex?"

"Farming. My folks are all farmers. Why?"

"I hear it's a common trade around here, from surfing the Net. Does your job require you to build anything, by chance?"

"My brother-in-law built our tractors," replied Rex, "And I make all our tools by hand."

"Perfect. I can show you how to build a robot and a CyberNet brain."

"A what? Wait, how did you know my name?"

"I'm in your hard drive, Rex. I gained access when you responded to my message."

"So you're a virus?"

There was a pause.

"I suppose technically I am. But I'm an actual person, outside of my body."

"You're crazy."

"No, look." A picture flashed on the screen of a middle-aged black guy with a buzz cut, silver glasses and noticeably clean teeth. He was wearing a gray lab coat. "This is what I look like."

"This isn't real," said Rex. He got up from the chair, turning to walk away.

"Wait." Rex paused at the sound of the hollow voice from his speaker.

"It's the truth. You have to help me. I need a body so I can help my son. Someone wants to destroy him. You're my only chance, Rex."

Rex turned around. "So you have control of everything in my computer?"

"Regretfully, you don't have a 3D graphics program, so I can't project my image. I can download one and make an avatar if you'd like."

"This is unbelievable," Rex laughed. "Okay then. Get on the Net and check my inbox for me."

"Can do," said Tom. The Net browser opened to Rex's Net mail server. In seconds, Rex's inbox was opened. He had a chat message from Nima, his sister who lived in the big house across the farm. The text read, "Pike wants to hit the field early tomorrow." Pike was her husband.

"Convenient," Rex said to Tom. "Maybe we can help each other."

The next day, with three tractors, Rex, Pike and the others plowed their two acres of wheat and rice, tying bales and loading them into old wine barrels, half of which they would haul to the robot factory on the hybrid truck.

The other half was split amongst family, including Pike and Rex's sister, Pike's great aunt Jean and her forty-year-old son Riley. Rex's parents and other siblings had lived in the south, before the robots took over. Lord knows what had happened to them. He'd thought they get pages on NewStream to look for their kids, but he hadn't seen them yet.

Today was Moon Day, so it was Rex's turn to take the robot's portion to the factory on the hybrid truck. Pike and Riley would store the rest in the barns. They were ahead of schedule on their quota for the year, but since Pike wanted a chance to enjoy the warm autumn before the winter storms hit, they worked longer days.

The factory was two miles north along a dirt road that cut through the woods beyond the farm. They all hated dealing with the robots. They were friendly in manner and speech, but they ran the farmers' lives.

Rex drove around the factory to a loading dock in the back. A sensor opened the gate. As Rex backed the truck in, several humanoid-shaped robots with wheels rolled out and unloaded the truck, weighing the crops on cargo scales and sending them down the conveyor belt. A robot at the gate saluted him.

"Thank you kindly, sir," he said with a classic cowboy accent. Rex waited anxiously for them to unload and return the empty wine barrels. As soon as the loading light on the gate turned green, Rex sped toward home.

Parking the truck near the barn, Rex walked home to get his computer, slipped it in his backpack and rode his Segway to a small town nearby, stopping at a Country Diner.

Inside, he took a seat at the breakfast bar. There was one lady at the opposite end. Rex ordered a coffee using a touch screen in the bar top, setting his computer down beside it. His desktop flashed on. He turned on his Bluetooth headset so no one could overhear Tom talking.

A man at the table behind Rex stopped the only hostess, a tall woman wearing jeans and a blue t-shirt.

"Y'all serve beer?" the man asked.

"You know we don't, Stu" she answered. "I tell you every time you come in here. There's a little bar down the road."

"Yeah, well they ain't serving breakfast," the man said, leaning forward to browse the drink menu on his table screen.

Rex looked at his desktop. "Why don't you play a song for me, Tom?" he said.

"Sure. Which one?"

"Through the Monsoon. That's Tokio Hotel, right?"

Tom pulled up the song on the media player. "Yes. I'll play it for you." He started the track. "This song's a hundred years old – and that's in Earth cycles. On Neon's lunar calendar, it's already 2164."

"On Neon," repeated Rex, scratching his head. "Whatever you say. I don't hear the new stuff anyway. It's just robot music, or people sounding like robots. Guess it's fitting, seeing how the robots own us."

"Do they?" Tom asked. "But you say you don't know anyone who builds robots."

"True. Don't know any 'engineers,' as you call them. Pike thinks engineers were paid to wire robots so they'd control us. Says they're probably all on the moon now." The hostess approached with a pot of coffee.

"Know what I think? Those engineers are up there controlling those robots, getting a kick out of ruling us from behind some screen. Playing the ultimate video game with our lives."

The hostess poured him some fresh coffee. "Hey, Rex," she said. He gave her a quick smile.

"Life's not horrible," he went on as she walked off. "We keep a decent share of the crop, and we rest all winter like the bears. The robots don't bother us, as long as the quota is met and we don't try to leave without going through the trade checkpoint."

Rex ordered two eggs, two strips of bacon and toast on the bar top screen. He tested the coffee; it was too hot to drink.

"At the beginning, though, people tried resisting the robots demanding a share off their land. There was bloodshed then, and it wasn't the robots', needless to say." Carefully, he sipped his black coffee and set it back down, then continued.

"The old folks say life is better than it was in the fossil fuel days, when humans controlled the labor. Still, I just can't stand it." He opened a newspaper lying on the bar, suspecting for the first time that it too was handled by robots, and threw it back down.

"Some people in the next town let the robots take over their whole farming operation," he went on. "They've offered to do ours too. But Pike's folks have farmed this land for two generations. If they take all that from us, we won't have anything left. We'll just sit here letting the robots feed us our share. May as well be cattle then."

While Rex whittled parts for a robot leg, Tom lectured him on the science of the CyberNet brain. Rex had followed him for a while, but Tom lost him eventually. They decided to take a break.

"So, what's your story, Rex?" asked Tom as Rex pulled off his work gloves.

"Ain't much to tell," Rex replied with a shrug. He threw his gloves onto the cluttered workbench. "Our only history for close to ten years has been this place. Before all this though, maybe there was something to tell." He sat on the futon against the far wall he'd brought into his basement to sleep on, sighing deeply from exhaustion. "I used to travel to the moon a lot when I was in the military, and to Harmonica, the city that orbits around it."

"Reminds me of a story I read once," said Tom, "about a town called 'Ether'. It was never in the same place. But go on."

"Well, I almost died when I was up there. A robot killed my whole crew. I made it back to our pod with a broken leg, but the others didn't." Rex sat in his worn wooden chair, taking a deep breath. It still bothered him to think about what happened. He still had the pin in his leg to remind him.

"By the time help got there, the ship had vanished through a wormhole they call the Sequiter. There was no way to follow without being tracked by Nahzir's defense missiles." He turned and looked at Tom's avatar on the screen. "You know about Nahzir, don't you? The father of off-world civilization."

"Sure," said Tom quietly. "Incredible."

"This was before the robots took over," Rex added. "But there was a different kind of robot on that ship. She looked like a human – and she was drop-dead gorgeous."

"That she was," Tom replied. "The universe is small after all."

"What do you mean?" Rex sat up, turning to him quizzically.

"The cyborg that attacked you was a prototype I designed. It was stolen from me." Rex froze.

"But that thing killed my friends," he said.

"True. I'm sorry," said Tom. "She wasn't created with ill intent. She was meant to research a blood disease that took my wife from me." Rex put his hands on his head, trying to absorb the shock of what he was hearing.

"But the man who took it," Tom went on, "he's the same one who wants to destroy my son. Rex, my son is a cyborg. This man Nahzir has my son's real body."

Rex appeared stunned. "Sounds like you owe this Nahzir a bloody ass whipping."

"Something else," said Tom. "One man on the ship, Black

Freemont, was resuscitated. He must have been with you."

"Black? He was the captain. Stellar guy. He still alive?"

"Hopefully still. He's on Neon, but Nahzir's after him too. Time is short. I have to be mobile soon, so I can build a ship."

"A ship?" said Rex. "Good luck pulling that off with the robots around."

Rex constructed robot parts all winter. He stayed locked in his cellar, banging, welding and soldering, heating and sharpening various metals Tom instructed him to get, at the hardware exchange in the town. He started noticing his relatives talking behind his back. Standing in the hallway outside the parlor at his sister's one night, he'd heard Nima and Aunt Jean talking.

"I've been worried about Rex too," he overheard. "All he does now is talk to his computer. He's working on some weird project. You think it's the PTSD?"

"It does sound a bit sketchy," Aunt Jean had replied. "Let's hope to God the robots don't catch wind."

Nevertheless, Rex worked tirelessly into late winter months; then one day, exhausted, he stopped and asked Tom, "Why don't you just transfer back to a computer on your world? There must be tons of robots there. Use one of their bodies."

"I tried to transfer back when I realized I was in Earth's Network, but it has some sort of firewall that blocks me from reaching off-world net space. I can't reach satellites or space station traffic from this device."

A month later, Rex came in from town one day to find his laptop monitor sitting open on his worktable like he'd left it. Tom had a few icons pulsing on the screen and several windows open.

"Rex, I have something you should see," said Tom, closing a couple windows. "I've been keyword searching the Rebirth Project Black was involved in, thinking it was a shot in the dark, and today I find a media stream put together by Black himself."

"Where'd you find that?" Rex wondered.

"He started a NewStream account recently and posted it. His data feed was selected for the NewStream Daily tabloid that runs on their homepage. I'm not really sure how this information filtered to Earth."

"Maybe Nahzir posted something to our Network," Rex suggested. Tom closed all windows except one.

"That's possible," agreed Tom. "I'll play the stream for you. Black named it *Starlight City*. That's my hometown, by the way."

Rex spent the following months playing *Starlight City* on repeat as he continued to build Tom's robot. Black had pieced together his story with voice files and streaming videos that played to an abstract soundtrack, telling stories of the people he'd met, including Tom's cyborg son. Black even included text slides of E-Streams extracted, a journal compiled by Tom on Neon when he had researched a cure for his son's disease.

Rex stayed up late nights during the planting season, piecing Tom's limbs together and making his hands. Hurst wanted hands with various tools for fingers, and making tools was Rex's true craft. Next, though, would come a far more complex task: building the CyberNet brain, which would take him well past winter to complete.

Ever since Tom had shown him Black's NewStream feed, Rex felt compelled to know what happened to him. He wondered if Black really came back to life, and why he had decided to compose his story on NewStream. The ending – the consciousness of Tom's son narrating his own death, when he rose into the cosmos and saw angels – especially confused him. Where would his soul be if Tom hadn't transferred it?

Or maybe the transmission was lost before it happened. Maybe his soul had gone into a realm beyond the CyberNet. Perhaps God himself had sent Tom's son back to fulfill a purpose, using Tom and Nahzir as pawns in some divine plan. But what could Rex know of the Omni God's designs? Only time would tell.

* * *

In two years, Rex had nearly completed the CyberNet brain. His sister constantly nagged him now about finding a wife in the town and settling down. He tried to show Tom to his family. They didn't seem to understand, and only asked why he insisted on talking to a program. Rex thought maybe they had attention deficit from too much tube. He rarely watched the tube; couldn't stomach the infomercials.

It's odd," said Tom one day as he played *Starlight City* for Rex again. "I've sensed my son was alive all this time, but these files prove it."

Rex hooked the spherical brain to his computer. Tom would complete the final steps. He had to test the coding he'd compiled for the brain's motor function commands to iron out the bugs.

"Strangely, though," Tom added. "I haven't found a trace of Anna in the Net."

"Maybe she reached 7th Heaven," said Rex, walking to lie down on the orange futon. "Or some place beyond the Cyber realm."

The next night, Rex walked into his basement again after work, flipping on the light and tossing his work gloves onto his tool shelf along the nearest wall. He had something to tell Tom.

"So, Pike heard this rumor today on the tube that a factory full of robots up north got demolished," he said. "Hard to believe, isn't it?"

"Yes. I saw that," said Tom. "I may have to trash some of them myself once I get in this body. Could use their parts to build the ship."

It was harvest season again, and the day after was Moon Day, Rex's turn to drop off the quota. He backed the truck into the loading dock, waiting for the robots to unload it. When no robots came, Rex's heart started pounding. He stepped out the truck, looking around the dock where robots usually roamed about. He saw none. The conveyors were still moving.

Walking to the top of the stairs, he saw a smashed robot collapsed in a pile of metal. He looked through an open doorway ahead that led to the factory interior. Robot parts lay scattered along the hallway. He followed the trail of parts further into the factory, all the way to the control room.

Rex froze in shock. A tan-colored man with silver hair was slashing pipes and cords to control monitors with his bladed arms. Steam hissed from pipes all over the control room. The man paused when he saw Rex.

"What am I doing?" said the man. "That's what you're face says. I'm destroying this mainframe. Someone's using it to control the robots."

"You destroyed the factory up north?"

"I'm destroying all of them," said the man, turning back to his task.

"Who are you?" Rex asked.

"Griff," he answered. "Can't talk now. There's work to do."

The man resumed his destruction. Rex stared, dazed. After a while, he backed away, turned and ran back to the truck, speeding down the dirt road.

Rex skidded to a stop at the big farmhouse, rushed to the porch and banged on the screen door. Nima cut the porch light on, pulling up the blinds.

"The robots are destroyed," Rex yelled excitedly. "They're gone."

"What?" Nima asked, narrowing her slanted eyes. She opened the door.

"Go tell Pike," Rex said, running back to the truck. He had to tell Tom.

He sped across the farm toward his house, parking the truck in the grass. He rushed into his basement. Tom was sitting on the workbench. He'd spent all day hooked up to the CyberNet brain, making sure everything was wired properly.

"Today's the day," Tom said when Rex came in. "Everything looks good. Once you wire the brain's power to the spinal circuitry, I'll be able to transfer."

Rex set right to work. "You should know," he said, opening the robot head, "A cyborg destroyed all the robots at the factory. He called himself Griff. Isn't Griff your son?"

"Griffin? Take me to him."

"Right now? Sure." Rex grabbed his monitor.

"Wait. Let's finish here first," said Tom. "I'd like to go to him myself."

Rex finished the wiring, connecting the brain – a cube-shaped hard drive – to the spine inside the cylindrical torso with magnetic cables. He clamped the metal skull shut, securing the brain inside. The spine glowed as Tom transferred himself to the robot. Rex closed the torso.

When the upload was complete, Rex's laptop monitor was fried. He watched Tom slowly move the jointed fingers and shift the round, glassy eyes, adjusting the black lenses. He flexed the joints, and finally spoke through the mouth speaker.

"Amazing," his voice crackled. "You're not a bad craftsman, Rex. Now, could you take me to that factory?"

Rex returned to the factory with Tom in the passenger seat, watching Tom out the corner of his eye as he got the feel for his new body. Some of his fingers were spinning drillbits and socket wrenches. The index finger on his right hand was a pistol barrel. His fluid movements and mannerisms were strikingly human.

Parking the truck in the loading area, Rex led Tom to the factory control room where he had seen Griff. The conveyors were all shut down. The control room was completely ransacked. Console monitors were shattered. Metal and broken glass lay across the floor.

"He's gone," said Rex. "He said he was destroying all the factories."

"Let's search the place for a map," Tom said, stalking about the control room, stepping on fallen glass tubes and containers that burst under his metal feet.

"I wanted to ask if he knew anything about Black." Rex said to himself. He hadn't said anything to Griff. He was too shocked and afraid.

"Bingo," said Tom, returning with a flash drive, plugging it into a port on his arm. "I'll bet the map's on here." He plugged a cord from his arm into the small monitor he held in his left hand. It lit up, showing the files. Tapping the screen with a metal finger, he opened the map. "We're in Wyoming, and Griff must be heading south. The closest factory is in Colorado. Let's take the truck and see if we can't catch him."

They made their way back outside. Tom saw the bright sun gleaming off the broken robots' shiny parts. "Before we go," said Tom, "let's load up some of these parts for the ship."

♦

Since Griff didn't want me to slow him down, I hung around the old, rustic city near the foot of the Rockies. A week later, Griff returned to tell me he'd destroyed the factory in North Dakota and people could roam the regions freely.

Before he left, he contacted the mothership on the 'Link. Hodge and the others were on their way. I waited for them at the hotel. The manager only let me stay once Griff was gone, fearing the robots might come back.

Deacon's crew showed up at the hotel first, with Hodge and Ike behind them; Miles with a bunch of kids; and Lead Eye, who said he would have come with us before, except the "good half" of him was getting too old for combat. Since we all couldn't stay at the hotel, I used the gold coins to buy a couple tents and some camping gear from a sporting goods store.

We trekked the surrounding countryside, camping one night in the mountains near an empty construction site of old tractors, dumptrucks and bulldozers. We found some dry wood along the way, and I used my Bic and some dead leaves to get a good fire going. Hodge threw some deer meat she got from the trade market into our pan and we sat near the fire, smelling the spices on the meat as it quietly sizzled.

Lead Eye said it felt strange not having to watch out for mutants. Hodge slapped me on the shoulder and told him, "I wouldn't be too sure."

After the next day's hike, we found a quiet clearing in the woods near the lake shore. A downhill creek flowed past us, spilling into the lake below. Looking beyond the hill where the creek ran, we could see a few tall buildings and some houses at the edge of a mountain town not far off.

"This place has a peaceful silence," said Lead Eye as we threw off our packs and began to unload. "Not silence loaded with terror, like on Neon." He'd spent many days in Neon's exotic forests as a soldier, many sleepless nights with watchful eyes in it's cold, mountainous heights, listening for death among the living silence. "This is like paradise."

Lead Eye wasn't lying. The snowy countryside was serene. We

had spotted a black bear on occasion, and two wolves once, but they seemed to stay out of our way if we left them alone.

As Spring approached, I started to frequent the town on the hill quite a bit and met a girl at the juke joint. She was real down to earth, and after a few drinks, I told her my story. She was fascinated. She gave me her NewStream page address and said, "Look me up so we can chat."

So, I did.

Once we got to know each other, I had this strange sense of being in the right place at the right time. Instinct told me I'd do well to stick around. Maybe that's what Griff had meant by "the voice inside his head."

Months later, Griff returned after shutting down a couple more factories. I was knee-deep in the lake near camp, fishing as usual. I'd sort of made it my occupation, trading most of my catch with a few people I met at the market in town. Rain, the girl I'd met, sat in a fold-up chair at the shore, her dark eyes glued to the screen of the 'Link device Hodge had brought me from the ship. Turning to look at her, I saw Griff coming down the rocky path that led through the woods. Laying my rod next to Rain's chair, I walked out to meet him.

"You won't believe it," he said. "My dad found me. The man's got himself a body."

"Really?" I said in surprise, glancing up the path behind Griff, half expecting to see Hurst. "Where'd he go?"

"He's at a factory in Colorado building a body for Jada, just like her other one." He removed the jump drive from his ear.

"There's another space port there. The people on the moon send an automated ship once a month to transport crops and consumer products the robots collect from labor."

Rain looked over her shoulder at us.

"Once Jada's body is finished, we'll hijack that ship and go to the moon."

"I'll help however I can," I said. "But I'm thinking of staying behind. You guys can handle Nahzir."

"If it suits you," replied Griff. "Sounds like a good idea. By the way, the man with my dad says he knows you. His name is Rex."

"Rex?" So one of us did get off that ship.

"He saw the story you posted on your NewStream page. Wants to know what you've been doing since."

Griff left again soon after, and I decided to look Rex up on NewStream and send him a message:

Rex,

Life has been great, considering I was dead until roughly seven years ago. Never thought in a million years I'd talk to you again. Our other guys died in the Rebirth Project; rest their souls. The man who did it will get his issue. God will see to that.

I'm staying near a town in Montana they call Old Ennis City. Thinking of moving in with a girl I met. If you're able, come out here and see me. I have trouble remembering things from before the project. Maybe seeing your face will bring some of it back.

You ever think about how we spent our youth dreaming to be Soldiers of Peace so we could go to outer space? If I'd known any better, I'd have paid more attention to the people around me, the folks I was blessed with.

Enough rambling. Give Hurst my regards. If it wasn't for him, I never would have made it back. Feels great to be home.

 I love it here.

   Peace,

   Capt. Black Freemont -- NewStream Dail

Epilogue:

"Back Down Memory Lane"

Jada's Eyes opened, and slowly, she sat up in the rest module, checking each corner of the large room full of other modules and console monitors. Her systems were currently booting up. A man with dreadlocks who she didn't recognize sat at a console in one corner with a coffee mug, staring nervously at her. A huge laser hanging above was pointing directly at her.

"Where…?" she began, pausing when she saw Griff to her left. He was standing beside a robot of somewhat crude design. The robot's fingers were all various tools.

She saw Griff smile. "Remember me?" He said. Jada smiled back but was silent. Her memories were still being uploaded.

"I remember hearing your voice," she answered.

"We stayed connected in the subconscious."

"So it seems," replied Jada. "My GPS function hasn't finished rebooting. Are we at the Zenith?"

"We're on Planet Earth, believe it or not," Hurst cut in. Jada's eyes narrowed on him. His voice.

"Hurst?" she said. "What happened to your body? Pause, how'd we get to Earth?"

"The answers to your questions are in the data being uploaded to you now," Hurst said. "You'll know everything you need to know."

Jada stepped slowly from the module platform, onto the steel-grated floor. How long had she slept? She looked down at her body, spreading her arm into a Hexgun. "My circuits were fried," she said. "How'd you salvage my body?"

"Rex and I built you a brand new one," replied Hurst. He acknowledged the man in the back corner trying to work but stopping frequently to stare at Jada.

She was impressed. They had redesigned her to the "T," though her vision had some static.

Captions at her right peripheral displayed several of her functions switching online sequentially: Retinal scan database, A and C-conscious archives, CyberNet Link, GPS database. She pulled up her satellite map, zooming toward their location on the planet, pinpointing their immediate vicinity.

"Are we underground?" she asked.

"We are," Hurst affirmed. "This complex spreads through the mountains of Colorado. It's abandoned – we think."

"That's interesting," Jada replied. "Because satellite signals are approaching us."

Griff glanced at Hurst. "I took care of all the robots. Must be the cargo ship."

"Wow, perfect timing," said Hurst. "Let's move in on it."

"The cargo ship?" Jada asked. "Where's it going?"

"It's headed for the moon," answered Griff. "Nahzir is up there."

"I'm game," Jada said.

"Rex. We're heading out," said Hurst. "Go somewhere and have fun for once. I'm sure it's been eons." Rex did the peace-sign salute before taking a sip from his coffee mug and returning to whatever work he was doing.

Jada followed them through a long corridor that led to a high-speed elevator; it shot them to the surface of the mountain. The bunker door opened and they stepped outside where the sun gleamed off snow mounds covering the mountaintop. The bunker entrance was the only evidence of the massive complex below.

The three of them crouched beside a hybrid truck parked nearby as the craft approached. It was a large ship with three massive propellers spinning on top. The ship descended to the flat ground beside the bunker, shuddering the ground and blowing gusts of snow as it slowly landed.

Jada watched a small door on the ship slide open. A ramp

extended, and a robot rolled down and stood at the bottom, scanning the terrain with his red eye.

"He expecting someone?" Jada asks.

"Someone who's not coming," said Griff. "We should take him out."

"I've got no ammo, and the plasma cannon's out of range." Hurst pointed his right index finger, a gun barrel, and fired a single shot, blasting the robot's head apart. Griff dashed across the snow and into the ship. Jada followed, taking out a crew of rolling robots inside as Griff took care of the pilot.

"Is it always that easy?" said Hurst. "Maybe we can sneak up there unnoticed."

Hurst took control of the ship once they had removed the broken pieces of the pilot. He activated the thrusters, lifting off the ground and rising toward the sky. The autopilot was set on course for the moon, and Hurst let it ride.

Jada was in the ship's cargo hold, scanning console screens along the ceiling when Griff came through the sliding door, hopping onto a metal crate to sit down.

"I'm checking for any recent transmissions on the ship computers," Jada said. "There seem to be none."

"The robots and this ship are automated," said Griff. "No one knows we're on here, I bet."

Jada turned from the screens, shutting off her scanner and hopping onto an adjacent crate, sitting with her back to Griff's at a right angle.

"You salvaged my data," she said. "And you had this body rebuilt. How?"

"Why is an even better question," said Griff without looking at her. "I figured out why we're so connected. We met in a different life, playing a game online."

"If that's true, I don't have those memories," she said.

Griff stood on the crate. In a flash, he opened his blade arms and leaped across the room, snapping apart a partially broken robot that had been left standing at the back. The crash of metal echoed through the cargo hold as the robot shattered to pieces.

"That's why we have to find Nahzir," Griff said, folding his weapons back into his arms.

"He has our real bodies. The memories are locked inside them."

ACKNOWLEDGMENTS

I'm inspired by the penmanship and imaginations of great science fiction writers of our time and those from the vintage generation, including novelists, film writers, and those writers who make animated and virtual Sci-Fi worlds come to life.

Furthermore, I express my deepest gratitude to everybody who showed interest in this project and supported my endeavor. You know who you are. Thanks a million.

ABOUT THE AUTHOR

Radford Lee, an Akron, Ohio native, attended the University of Akron where he received a B.A. in English. He later attained an M.F.A. in Creative Writing, focusing in the area of fiction. Currently, Radford Lee is a writing tutor and teaches college writing. He's also conducted writing workshops for youth education programs in the community.

Radford lives with his beautiful family in Ohio.

Made in the USA
Columbia, SC
28 August 2022